Every word I have written and published is from my noggin (brain, in case you don't know what noggin means). My fiction is all make-believe, from the deep dive into my wild imagination. All my nonfiction books have been researched until my brain has scrambled.

I0571774

Nonfiction	
The Puppy Baby Book	Maste
Puppy Adoption and Beyond	Writers
Mastering Your Money (2008)	What's
Online Classes	
Writers Preparation Handbook	How to Format Word Docs Like A Pro
Cozy Mysteries	**Sci-Fi-Fantasy**
The Alcott Family Adventures	**The Thol Series**
Hot Chocolate	Prophecy of Thol
Bitter Chocolate	Gifts From Thol
Spicy Chocolate	Love of Thol
Nutty Chocolate	King of Thol
Katz' Cat Series	Earth Calling Thol
Katz' Cat	**Sci-Fi Romance Adventure**
Bill Hill's Pills	Forced Dreams
The Detectives	**Dystopian**
The Pact	The Last Dog
Discreet Conversations	Texmexzona
Books by my Alter Ego ~ DG Ireland	
Bonded Shapeshifter Billionaire Series	
Bonded	
Tothars	
Tilted	
Unforeseen	
Connected	
Need A Notebook?	
See my 54 themed notebooks on my website www.degreenfield.com/notebooks	
Screenplays formatted as books	
Plan B (Dark Comedy)	Where's Ralphie? (Family Comedy)
The God Child (Action Adventure)	Standing Dead (Drama/Tragedy)
The Far Corner (Sci-Fi/Psychological/Creatures)	Block Captain (Action Comedy)
Screenplays as TV Episodes	
Hot Chocolate ~ Episode 1	Prophecy of Thol ~ Episode 1
Bonded ~ Episode 1	
See my screenplays and awards on my website: degreenfield.com Filmfreeway, ISA Network	

Standing Dead by Dawn Greenfield Ireland

Published by Artistic Origins

Copyright © 2026 by Dawn Greenfield Ireland

Cover by JewelDSign, Fiverr.com

Interior layout by Yours Truly (me), Corrections 6/1/2026

ISBN 9781940385990 (eBook)

Dawn Greenfield Ireland

Artistic Origins

www.degreenfield.com

Publisher's Note: This is a work of fiction. Names, characters, places, and incidents are a product of the author's imagination. Locales and public names are sometimes used for atmospheric purposes. Any resemblance to actual people, living or dead, or to businesses, companies, events, institutions, or locales is completely coincidental.

This book may contain references to specific commercial products, process or service by trade name, trademark, manufacturer, or otherwise, specific brand-name products and/or trade names of products, which are trademarks or registered trademarks and/or trade names, and these are property of their respective owners. Dawn Greenfield Ireland or her associates, have no association with any specific commercial products, process, or service by trade name, trademark, manufacturer, or otherwise, specific brand-name products and/or trade names of products.

Please visit my website: www.degreenfield.com and sign up for my newsletter and get the latest news before the public.

✿ Formatted with Vellum

STANDING DEAD

SCREENPLAY IN BOOK FORMAT

DAWN GREENFIELD IRELAND

ARTISTIC
ORIGINS

CONTENTS

READING A SCREENPLAY

About Screenplays...

This is one of my screenplays that I have adapted into book format. The number of pages from script to book format changed due to the formatting characteristics of the publishing program to create eBooks and paperbacks.

In case you are not familiar with the elements of a script, I'll give you a boost so you enjoy reading these pages.

FADE IN: opens the screenplay.

INT. means any interior scene, such as a room, building, barn—anywhere inside.

EXT. means any exterior scene, such as outside on the grass, outside of the car, house — you get it, right?

When a character is first introduced, their name appears in all capital letters. After that, the name is displayed as normal.

Each character's action is in a separate paragraph.

Character dialog in a screenplay is tricky in this format. The character's name is in the center of the page, then the dialogue is inset at the left margin under the name.

I've done my best with the formatting, but it isn't perfect. You will notice that the dialogue and character names are centered.

FADE OUT. This is the end of the script.

If you have questions, suggestions, or tips, send me an email: dawn@degreenfield.com, but don't spam me.

LOGLINE AND SYNOPSIS

Standing Dead

★ WINNER: WOMEN IN FILM & TELEVISION / HOUSTON REEL DIALOGUES ★

LOGLINE:

When a tightly knit group of college friends climbs the corporate ladder of success, a lifetime of unchecked infidelity, greed, and deception unravels after a tragic death—leaving one man to watch his perfect life collapse under the weight of his own secrets.

SYNOPSIS:

Jealousy. Lies. Greed. Desire.

Alex, Chelsea, Phillip, and Donna are inseparable college friends whose lives are tightly woven together. But in an era where being a little too naïve carries a devastatingly high price, their bond is built on a foundation of shifting sand.

Alex and Phillip have been best friends since high school, roommates through college, and masters of deception. Neither knows the definition of being faithful, and both have turned lying into an art form.

Graduation brings the success they always craved: dental school for Chelsea, advertising for Phillip, law school for Donna, and a lucrative stock brokerage career for Alex. But when Alex marries Chelsea, Phillip is named best man—while secretly burning with a quiet, dangerous resentment.

As the years pass, the corner offices get bigger, the babies arrive, and the affairs multiply. The group hides their betrayals behind a mask of perfect, upper-class normalcy.

Until the unthinkable happens.

When Phillip suddenly falls ill and dies, the tightly woven web of deceit begins to unravel thread by thread. With the ultimate buffer gone, the truths behind years of stolen moments and financial greed begin to bleed into the light.

Chelsea is forced to face a horrifying reality about the man she married; a sick child requires desperate measures, and Alex is left standing in the wreckage of a life built entirely on lies.

Standing Dead is a prestigious, deeply moving tragedy about the devastating ripple effects of betrayal, the cost of ambition, and the heartbreaking truth that some secrets can kill.

Scroll up and grab your copy to witness the unraveling today.

Standing Dead

Jealousy, lies, greed, and desire... Alex discovers too late that secrets can kill.

FADE IN:

EXT. CEMETERY - CURRENT DAY

Granite angels with arms outspread, cherubs with adoring gazes, Celtic, Calvary, Patriarchal and Latin crosses and other beautiful headstones rise up amid meandering walkways.

GROUNDS PEOPLE tend to the manicured landscape, trimming, clipping, raking. Birds sing.

Forty MOURNERS suffer in the heat and humidity.

A somber canopy protects the PRIEST, coffin, immediate FAMILY and CLOSE FRIENDS who sit on wooden folding chairs.

The remaining MOURNERS wilt as the sun beats down on their black attire as they stand in small clusters.

Flowers and a large cross adorn the coffin.

                    PRIEST (B.G.)
Our brother Phillip has gone to his rest in the peace of Christ. May the Lord now welcome him to the table of God's children in heaven. With faith and hope in eternal life, let us assist him with our prayers.

ALEX, 32, a self-centered, highly successful stockbroker, captures hearts with a mere glance and tosses them away.

His face masks controlled emotion as he holds JASON, 4, his sandy-haired miniature replica, twisting to get down.

CHELSEA, 30, Alex' wife, stands beside him, elegant, yet very sensitive as she wipes tears from her face.

A successful dentist in an upscale setting, Chelsea followed in her parent's footsteps.

JANIE, 2, already showing signs of independence, sleeps on Chelsea's shoulder as Chelsea gently sways.

Chelsea shifts Janie to untangle her shoulder-length sandy hair.

She stares into space over the coffin, lips quivering as she tries to hold back tears.

ALEX (V.O.)
Who would have thought that the passing of your best friend would dramatically have you reexamining every aspect of your relationship with that person?

Alex gazes at the coffin and closes his eyes, a pained expression flashes across his face.

EXT. PARK - DAY - LATE 1980s

A YOUNGER ALEX, 22, solid as a rock without even trying, in raggedy t-shirt and sweat pants, runs and passes a football.

PHILLIP, 23, pinup from the word go with his dark hair and brooding eyes - totally aware of his charm - stretches and catches the ball.

Adorned with heavy gold ID bracelet and neck chain, he's manicured and wealthy.

A YOUNGER CHELSEA, 20, book-bag by her feet, and DONNA, 23, someone you wouldn't forget easily, cheer them on, along with other college GIRLS.

ALEX (V.O.)
Phillip and I had been friends since high school.

Phillip stumbles and rolls with the fall, then leaps back up on his feet and charges toward Alex.

PHILLIP
Ninety-two coming through!

The girls laugh.

Alex tries to avoid him, but gets caught by Phillip's forward thrust.

Both go down.

Alex lands on his back with Phillip half covering him.

ALEX
Move your dead carcass off me.

Phillip laughs and rolls to the side, then flops over on his back, holding his jaw.

PHILLIP
I need a dentist!

Chelsea comes over and plops down on Phillip.

Phillip GRUNTS in pain.

PHILLIP
It's not fair to do that when a man's suffering.

CHELSEA
Open.

Phillip opens his mouth.

Chelsea pokes around inside.

CHELSEA
Molar is a little loose. It will be okay, but you need to make
sure you give it a rest for several days. Eat on the other
side.

DONNA
Want to sue him Phillip? I'll take the case pro bono.

ALEX
I'm clearly outnumbered.

Chelsea gets up and hauls Phillip to his feet.

DONNA
You guys going to the rally tonight?

ALEX
We will be there, my beauties.

Donna and the girls giggle and walk away.

Chelsea lingers behind.

ALEX (V.O.)

There wasn't a girl alive who could resist our charm or good
looks.

DONNA

Phillip! Don't forget you owe me a beer!

Phillip waves and offers one of his heart melting smiles.

CHELSEA

Alex, did you ask Phillip about tomorrow night?

Alex gets up. He cringes.

Phillip waits, expectantly.

PHILLIP

What are we doing tomorrow night?

ALEX

Brandon White's gallery opening.

CHELSEA

Plus Donna, so we can be a foursome.

PHILLIP

Yeah, count me in.

CHELSEA

Great! Got to run.

Alex' gaze follows Chelsea as she sprints off to a car.

PHILLIP

Chelsea and Donna, again?

ALEX
We're not in high school anymore, Phillip.

Alex shoves his elbow into Phillip.

Phillip grunts from the impact. They walk to an apartment and enter.

INT. APARTMENT - DAY - LATE 1980s

It's obvious these two aren't working their way through college.

Alex strips off his shirt as he crosses the living room and enters the bathroom.

The shower water comes on.

Phillip turns the stereo on then disappears into a bedroom.

INT. BATHROOM - DAY - LATE 1980s

Phillip walks in, naked.

ALEX (V.O.)
But then everyone has secrets.

Alex, slightly visible through the opaque shower curtain, stretches against the wall as the water cascades.

Phillip smiles, parts the curtain and enters the tub.

INT. CLASSROOM - DAY - LATE 1980s

A PROFESSOR, 55, writes on the blackboard as he drones.

PROFESSOR

This paper will count for sixty-five percent of your final grade. If you've taken good notes, you'll have it made. If not, I'll see you next semester.

Alex, Phillip and Chelsea sit among the STUDENTS.

Alex and Chelsea whisper to each other.

> CHELSEA
> Did you finish the history paper?

> ALEX
> Almost. What'll you give me for it?

> CHELSEA
> Whatever you want darling, but I won't stand in line.

> ALEX (V.O.)
> I knew Chelsea was the woman I'd marry from the first moment I saw her.

Alex playfully snaps his teeth at her.

Chelsea giggles.

Phillip watches, angry and jealous.

EXT/INT. CAR - DAY - LATE 1980s

Alex drives.

Phillip's face is contorted with rage. The car pulls up to the apartment complex.

Phillip gets out and slams the door. He rushes upstairs, goes inside and slams the apartment door.

Alex sits in the car for a moment, his face tight with tension, then goes into the apartment.

INT. APARTMENT - NIGHT - LATE 1980s

Alex and Phillip lie in bed, a large gap between them.

Alex stares at the ceiling. He glances at Phillip.

Alex turns on his side toward Phillip, puts his arm around his waist and gently moves close to Phillip.

Alex kisses Phillip's neck and shoulder. His hand caresses Phillip's hip.

Phillip's hand covers Alex' hand and follows his motions.

Alex buries his face in Phillip's hair.

INT. CHELSEA'S APARTMENT - AFTERNOON - LATE 1980s

Chelsea jogs briskly on a treadmill in her spare bedroom while Alex puts the Nordic Rider through its paces.

Hand weights on a stand are among the chrome exercise equipment crowded into the small room.

Chelsea turns a page on a book propped on the treadmill and laughs.

CHELSEA
I wish they'd make a movie out of this book.

ALEX
What is it?

CHELSEA

Confederacy of Dunces.

ALEX
I knew you'd like it.

Alex takes a break and swigs water. He drinks in Chelsea.

EXT. CEMETERY - CURRENT DAY

Alex appears somewhat dazed.

Chelsea touches his arm.

He turns and takes Janie.

Alex glances around.

His gaze rests on CHAYNE, 30, well-dressed, sophisticated; a
picture-perfect mourner.

EXT. PARK - DAY - LATE 1980s

A YOUNGER CHAYNE, 22, jogs along a park trail, ponytail
bobbing, looking to score a man.

Alex, 22, warms up with stretches. He notices Chayne as she
passes, and bounds off after her.

Alex catches up with Chayne, checks her out, then
passes her.

Chayne sprints after Alex, like a dog in heat.

Alex jogs off the trail onto the grass, slows down, then rolls onto
the ground, breathes hard.

Chayne follows, stops at Alex' feet and smiles down at him.

Alex returns the smile and stretches out his arm to Chayne.
Chayne grabs Alex' arm and pulls him to his feet.

They walk off together.

INT. APARTMENT - AFTERNOON - LATE 1980s

Alex enters, a towel across his shoulders.

Phillip enters the room from the kitchen.

PHILLIP
Where the hell have you been?

Alex rubs the back of his neck with the towel.

ALEX
Running; what's your problem?

PHILLIP
You left three hours ago!

Alex goes into the bathroom and tosses the towel in the hamper, Phillip on his heels.

ALEX
Do I have to account for every moment I'm away from you?
Christ, give me a break.

PHILLIP
You're supposed to cook tonight, did you forget? And Chelsea's called twice wanting to know what time to be here.

ALEX
It's five-thirty. Dinner's in two hours.

PHILLIP

Are you seeing someone else?

Alex pushes past Phillip and goes to the kitchen.

The makings for supper are on the counter.

> PHILLIP
> You didn't answer.

> ALEX
> What is this, a trust issue? This conversation replays every time
> I go out the door.

Phillip appears guilty.

> PHILLIP
> Shit. I'm sorry.

Alex moves to in back of Phillip and massages his shoulders.

> ALEX
> At least I know you still love me.

He kisses Phillip's neck.

Phillip closes his eyes with desire.

INT. APARTMENT - NIGHT - LATE 1980s

Chelsea, Phillip and Alex sit at the table munching on salad.

> PHILLIP
> I've got an interview tomorrow.

> CHELSEA

That big ad agency?

                    ALEX
Yeah, he's going to take us all out to dinner if he gets
                   the job.

Phillip raises his beer in a toast.

                  PHILLIP
                 (to Alex)
You better hope someone offers you a job.

                    ALEC
I don't have to worry about getting a job... Chelsea can always
                 support me.

                  CHELSEA
Dentists do make great money.

All share a laugh.

                  PHILLIP
Want to go dancing?

Alex and Chelsea don't appear enthusiastic.

                    ALEX
How about a movie?

Chelsea wrinkles her nose.

                  CHELSEA
Nah. I want to finish reading my book.

INT. GAY NIGHTCLUB - NIGHT - LATE 1980s

The PACKED club swings.

Phillip, drink in hand, and a GUY dance to a fast beat. Electricity flows between the two dancers.

The tune ends and another begins. Phillip and the Guy never miss a beat.

> GUY
> You here with someone?

> PHILLIP
> My roommate's studying.

The Guy appears hurt.

> GUY
> So you're not available?

Phillip coyly smiles.

> PHILLIP
> Who said I wasn't?

They leave the dance floor, mid tune, and head for the front door, arm in arm.

INT. RESTAURANT - DAY - LATE 1980s

Phillip sits at a table with Chelsea and Donna.

A napkin rests on the fourth chair.

Chelsea holds court on the conversation.

CHELSEA

Six more weeks until graduation. Then off to dental school.

DONNA

When are you leaving?

CHELSEA

August first. I've got to find an apartment and I want to take my time finding my way around San Antonio, the campus, and the River Walk.

DONNA

Are you sure you want to spend another four years in school?

CHELSEA

What do you expect... both my parents are dentists. It's in my blood.

DONNA

It's off to law school for me. I want a deal like my dad.

Phillip watches Alex across the room, oblivious to the conversation.

CHELSEA

He made partner in two years, didn't he?

DONNA

It helps when you're wealthy.

CHELSEA

You can be so shallow.

DONNA

You ever need a lawyer, I'll rep you for free.

Phillip comes out of his daze.

PHILLIP

Will you represent me too, Donna?

DONNA

That depends...

Donna winks.

PHILLIP

Whoa... your rates are high!

Alex comes back to the group, picks up his napkin and sits.

CHELSEA

Spreading your good news?

ALEX

Passing out cards to prospective clients.

PHILLIP

Yeah, I guess every Tom, DICK and Harry.

Alex glares at Phillip, then turns to the girls.

ALEX

My father can't spare the beer money for my masters degree, so
I need to hustle.

Chelsea and Donna glance quizzically from Alex to Phillip.

INT. APARTMENT - DAY - LATE 1980s

Alex, in shorts, t-shirt and barefooted, sits on one end of the couch, books spread out around him.

Phillip, dressed similarly, sits on the other end of the couch with books and lined tablets.

Phone rings. Alex picks up the receiver, distracted. He glances at the clock: 1:00.

> ALEX
> Hello?

> CHAYNE (V.O.)
> My hot tub is calling out to you.

Alex sneaks a glance toward Phillip.

> ALEX
> I'm working on my philosophy paper.

His eyes dart over to Phillip.

Phillip continues to study.

> ALEX
> I'll run it over to you later, okay?

> CHAYNE (V.O.)
> About an hour and a half?

> ALEX

Can you wait that long?

CHAYNE (V.O.)
Cute.

Phillip marks his place.

PHILLIP
Who was that?

ALEX
Mel. He can't find his math book so I'm going to loan him mine.
I'll drop it off when I go for a run.

PHILLIP
That dork couldn't find his mother in that pigsty.

They return to their studies.

LATER

Alex gets off the couch and stretches. He glances at the clock:
2:30.

Phillip continues to study.

ALEX
I need a break. I'm going for a run.

PHILLIP
Good idea. Think I'll head for the pool.

Phillip stretches, goes to the kitchen and returns with a towel
and plops it on the back of the couch.

Alex goes to the bedroom and returns with running shoes and socks in hand.

He flops down on the couch and puts his socks and shoes on, then exits.

Phillip notices the book, grabs it and bolts off the couch and tears the door open.

EXT. APARTMENT - DAY - LATE 1980s

Phillip darts to the railing.

Alex stretches downstairs.

>   PHILLIP
>   Alex! The math book!

Alex' head jerks up, remembers.

>   ALEX
>   Shit.

Alex climbs the stairs to get the book.

>   ALEX
>   I never would have heard the end of it. See you later.

Phillip leans against the railing and watches as Alex bounds off, book in hand.

EXT. APARTMENT - DAY - LATE 1980s

Phillip, towel in hand, emerges from the apartment ready for a swim. He's slick with tanning oil.

He descends the stairs and heads to the pool.

EXT. POOL SIDE - LATE 1980s

Several MEN and WOMEN sun and swim.

Phillip enters the pool area, grabs a lounge chair and gets situated in a vacant spot.

He drapes the towel on the chair, takes his shoes off.

All eyes watch him as he settles in the chair.

PHILLIP'S P.O.V - THE SUNBATHERS

A YOUNG COUPLE in the pool, wrapped around each other.

A MAN, 50, swims laps.

TWO COUPLES sit on the pool stairs chatting.

A WOMAN dozes on a lounge chair, all greased up.

A YOUNG GUY sits beside a YOUNG WOMAN talking animatedly.

DAVID, 26, a muscular, blond, stares boldly at Phillip from a lawn chair directly opposite him.

BACK TO SCENE

Phillip slips the sunglasses down his nose and returns the stare.

David smiles lazily.

Phillip smiles back, replaces his glasses and gets comfortable.

LATER

Phillip wakes, gets up and goes into the water.

David swims laps.

Phillip wades out directly in his path.

David stops, stands, slings his hair back, splashing Phillip. He smiles widely.

Phillip smiles.

PHILLIP
Do you approve?

DAVID
Oh... yes.

He extends his hand.

DAVID
David.

Phillip grasps his hand.

PHILLIP
Phillip. Just move in?

DAVID
Six months. Keep to myself mostly.

PHILLIP
Anti-social or busy life?

David laughs lightly.

DAVID
Studying, working part-time, working out.

PHILLIP
No time for fun, huh?

DAVID
Working out is fun. Haven't had much of a social life in a while
though.

PHILLIP
That's not good.

DAVID
Got a remedy?

Phillip smiles suggestively.

INT. APARTMENT - AFTERNOON - LATE 1980s

Phillip sits on the couch eating pasta. Books and papers are
spread out around him; a bowl of pasta sits on the coffee table.

In the b.g. the clock shows 5:30.

The front door opens, Alex enters with a bottle of wine.

ALEX
You cooked.

PHILLIP
Neighbor brought it over.

ALEX
Really?

He holds up the wine.

PHILLIP
Grab it while it's still hot.

ALEX
Want some wine?

Phillip nods.

Alex sets the wine on the coffee table, then heads for the kitchen.

ALEX
Did you go to the pool?

Phillip eats with gusto.

PHILLIP
Yeah. It was pretty crowded.

Alex returns with a plate, a couple of paper towels, and two wine glasses.

He scoops pasta onto his plate and flops down on the couch and digs in.

INT. BEDROOM - NIGHT - LATE 1980s

A wracking cough shatters the silence. The rustle of bed covers.

ALEX
You okay?

Coughing.

PHILLIP

Shouldn't have gone swimming. Damn bronchitis must have kicked in.

Phillip coughs in succession.

ALEX
Any more stuff left?

PHILLIP
A little.

Alex turns on the light and gets up. He walks across to the bathroom and turns the light on.

The light goes off and Alex returns with a bottle. He gets in bed and hands the bottle to Phillip.

Phillip takes the cap off and chugs a mouthful. He replaces the cap and puts the bottle on the night stand.

PHILLIP
Thanks.

Phillip lies back down.

Alex shuts off the light and lies back down.

EXT. COLLEGE CAMPUS - DAY - LATE 1980s

Alex and Phillip walk across the grounds, backpacks strapped on.

David walks toward them, recognizes Phillip, smiles, and calls out to him.

DAVID

Hey, neighbor.

Phillip smiles at David as they approach.

PHILLIP
Hi, David.

All stop and shake hands.

PHILLIP
This is my roommate, Alex. Alex, this is David, he lives in our complex.

Alex glances from Phillip to David.

ALEX
Really? When did you two meet?

DAVID
Just the other day at the pool. Did you like the pasta I made?

Alex nods, a tight smile on his face.

ALEX
It was great. Thanks.

DAVID
I'd better get going, have to make my science class.

Phillip coughs.

PHILLIP
Yeah, we'd better get our butts in gear too.

Phillip and David jostle each other playfully as they go their own ways.

Alex walks in silence for a couple of beats.

> ALEX
> You didn't tell me you met someone at the pool.

> PHILLIP
> Must have slipped my mind.

> ALEX
> Hard to forget something like good food.

They continue walking.

Alex' face is strained.

Phillip beams.

Chelsea and Donna approach on a path diagonal to the guys. Chelsea notices them first.

> CHELSEA
> Hey, wait up.

The guys see the girls and stop.

Chelsea and Donna trot up to them.

> CHELSEA
> I've got a date with Greg Richards tonight!

> ALEX
> Cheating on me, huh?

Chelsea pokes Alex.

                    DONNA
At least someone has a prospect. Where are you going?

                    CHELSEA
Dinner and a play.

                    DONNA
Culture. How romantic.

Alex' face tightens as he withdraws from the conversation.

                    PHILLIP
What's the play?

                    CHELSEA
Something about angles and a boy who was murdered in
Mississippi.

                    PHILLIP
That's Norris and John's play. Very dramatic.

                    DONNA
Dramatic? It's hard to watch.

                    PHILLIP
You're just too high strung.

                    DONNA
Oh really, big boy. Don't tell me it didn't affect you.

Chelsea glances at her watch.

CHELSEA
Tick tock.

They pair up and walk away in silence.

EXT. COLLEGE CAMPUS - DAY - LATE 1980s

The grounds are packed for the graduation ceremony.

PEOPLE sit on folding chairs.

STUDENTS march up to get their diplomas, one by one, shake hands with the DEAN, and return to their places.

Alex, Phillip, Chelsea, Donna, David and Chayne are scattered throughout the graduating body.

The ceremonies end amidst claps, cheers, and the band plays on.

Graduation caps fly through the air.

Alex finds Phillip. They hug and slap each other on the back. They are joined by Chelsea, then Donna.

They all exchange hugs and kisses.

Donna furiously snaps pictures with her Nikon.

Alex kisses Chelsea, passionately.

CHELSEA
We should have graduated long ago.

Alex winks.

David wanders over and he and Phillip embrace heavily.

Everyone else continues with post-graduating high.

Chayne wanders over nonchalantly and congratulates Alex with a devouring kiss as Chelsea looks on and the others gawk.

> CHAYNE
> You do look good in a hat.

Alex laughs and introduces her.

> ALEX
> Everyone, I'd like you to meet Chayne. This is Phillip, my roommate, Chelsea, Donna, David - right?

David nods as he grasps Chayne's hand.

> CHAYNE
> The world awaits us... after we pay homage to our parents for this wonderful education.

All laugh lightly.

> ALEX
> Let us bow our heads in thanks.

He bows his head in mock seriousness.

> CHAYNE
> I'm off. It's banquet time. I'll see YOU later.

Chayne leaves, winding through the crowd. All eyes are riveted on Alex.

> ALEX
> She's a little strange.

Chelsea watches Chayne's departure through the crowd.

CHELSEA
No comment. Let's go get the folks and get out of here. I've got
steaks marinating.

DAVID
Guess I'll see you later.

David turns to leave.

Chelsea grabs his sleeve.

CHELSEA
Why don't you come over. I've got plenty.

David appears embarrassed.

PHILLIP
Yeah, come on, it'll be fun.

Alex looks from Phillip to David.

ALEX
The more the merrier.

DONNA
I'll catch up with you later. I've got one stop to make.

Alex throws his arm across Chelsea's shoulder and propels her
forward.

Chelsea goes with the flow and hooks her arm across Alex'
lower back.

Phillip appears confused.

David beams.

INT. CHELSEA'S APARTMENT - AFTERNOON - LATE 1980s

Chelsea's place is a jungle with plants and fresh cut flowers.

Through the sliding glass patio door, Alex, his PARENTS and CHELSEA'S FATHER are at the grill, which overlooks the CROWDED, noisy pool.

Alex tends to the food.

Chelsea plays hostess as she hands out beers and cokes from a tray.

About a dozen PEOPLE mingle, including Phillip and David.

The door opens and Donna enters, toting a shopping bag. She joins Chelsea, Phillip and David.

> DONNA
> Present time.

> CHELSEA
> Wait a minute!

Chelsea sets the tray on an end table, disappears into another room and returns with gifts.

Donna and Chelsea pass out gifts to each other and Phillip.

> CHELSEA
> David, I wish I had known you were going to be here...

DAVID
Hey, this is fun.

Chelsea glances to the patio.

CHELSEA
Should I go get Alex?

DONNA
In a minute. Open it.

Chelsea opens Donna's gift.

It's a framed picture collage with pictures dating back to when they were in elementary school together, plus high school and a picture of the graduation ceremony that day.

CHELSEA
Oh my God! Fourth grade when we met!

Chelsea and Donna hug.

Phillip rips open his gift wrappings, with David close to his side.

Chelsea grabs Donna by the arm and motions for Phillip and David to follow. They enter the spare bedroom.

INT. CHELSEAS BEDROOM - DAY - LATE 1980s

A bulky white box sits on the seat of the Nordic Rider.

CHELSEA
Look what my mom gave me. She and dad didn't think paying

for my undergrad education was enough... plus footing the bill for dental school.

She leads them to the box where a compact stair-stepper waits to be unpacked.

DONNA
A stair-stepper! You were going to order one!

DAVID
Now I know where to come when the gym is closed.

PHILLIP
Getting kind of crowded in here, isn't it Chelsea?

Phillip caresses the Nordic Rider.

CHELSEA
Don't even think about it.

Chelsea swats at Phillip.

He dodges the hit.

They exit the room, giggling.

Chelsea retrieves the tray.

CHELSEA
I'd better get busy before my mom...

Chelsea's MOTHER relieves the tray from her.

CHELSEA'S MOM

Alex is stuck in parent hell.

She propels Chelsea toward the sliding door with one hand and balances the tray with the other hand.

CHELSEA
He'll be okay, you'll see.

PHILLIP
Yeah, Alex hasn't sent any rescue signals yet.

They laugh.

Chelsea's father enters the apartment.

CHELSEA'S FATHER
We're ready for the corn.

CHELSEA
Great.

Chelsea heads to the kitchen, her parents follow.

INT. CHELSEAS KITCHEN - DAY - LATE 1980s

Chelsea grabs the platter of foil-wrapped corn and hands it to her dad.

He exits the kitchen.

The counter is filled with chip bags, pickle jars, etc.

CHELSEA'S MOM
Alex is very nice, Chelsea.

Chelsea grabs a sponge and wipes off the counter.

CHELSEA
We're just friends, Mom.

CHELSEA'S MOM
Now dear, you've been dating him for years. Your father and I
think...

CHELSEA
Mom, we were in college together. I've dated Greg, John, and
Joe Simon; remember them?

She stops and faces her mother.

CHELSEA
Don't try to plan my life, Mom. I've got another four years of
school and Alex is going for his Masters. Then I plan on
developing my career and making a solid foundation before I
begin thinking about marriage and babies.

CHELSEA'S MOM
Your father and I are simply interested in your welfare.

CHELSEA
Oh cut it out, Mom. It's not like I'm some poor, mousy little
thing who needs help. Alex and I are just friends, we've never
even been to bed together.

Chelsea's mother appears shocked.

Phillip enters the kitchen, David in tow.

PHILLIP
Want us to set the table?

Chelsea puts her arms around him and gives him a peck on the lips.

CHELSEA
You're too sweet, Phillip. Tell you what, you and David can set the table and I'll do something with the rest of this stuff.

David's face beams.

DAVID
If you don't think it's too pushy of me, how about if we switch jobs. I'm pretty handy with this.

PHILLIP
Talk about modesty, David worked his way through school as a chef.

Chelsea curtsies and backs off.

CHELSEA
Come on, Mom, we both know this isn't our territory.

Chelsea grabs dishes out of a cabinet; her Mom opens a drawer and gets silverware and they exit the kitchen.

David begins work as Phillip watches.

INT. CHELSEA'S APARTMENT - NIGHT - LATE 1980s

The otherwise dark apartment is bathed in light from the pool area.

Alex and Chelsea, sprawled in each other's arms, make out on the sofa.

INT. GAY NIGHTCLUB - NIGHT - LATE 1980s

Phillip and David dance to a slow number as tight as ticks, oblivious to the DANCERS around them.

INT. ALEX AND PHILLIP'S APARTMENT - DAY - LATE 1980s

Alex and Phillip sit on the edge of the sofa hunched over a map on the coffee table.

Phillip draws circles on the map with a blue highlighter.

PHILLIP
Here's my office building and our apartment.

Alex searches.

Phillip butts in and makes another circle.

PHILLIP
Here you go.

They study the map in silence.

ALEX
That's at least a forty-five minute drive.

Alex turns to Phillip.

ALEX
Looks like we're moving in different directions after all these years.

Phillip appears strained.

> **PHILLIP**
>
> Why don't we just move to a more centrally located place?

> **ALEX**
>
> We've stretched it this year, don't you think?

Phillip languishes in denial.

> **PHILLIP**
>
> It's natural to have disagreements with the stress of preparing for graduation.

> **ALEX**
>
> Phillip, I know about David. It's obvious.

> **PHILLIP**
>
> Alex, you'll always be first and foremost in my life, no matter who I'm with.

Both ponder.

EXT. CEMETERY - CURRENT DAY

Janie yanks on Alex' pant leg.

He stoops and picks her up; kisses her cheek.

Chelsea brushes a wisp of hair out of Jason's face. She glances across the faces in the crowd.

Alex' parents are present and somber.

Alex meets David's blank stare across the coffin.

David appears haggard and thin.

Alex suffers as he watches David.

Donna stands by Chelsea's side, crying openly.

Chelsea grabs Donna's hand.

EXT. MOVIE THEATER - NIGHT - LATE 1980s

A younger Alex and Chelsea exit the theater in deep discussion.

> CHELSEA
> I am not a prude.

> ALEX
> They're breasts, for Christ sake. What's the big deal?

Chelsea stops in mid step.

> CHELSEA
> You don't see men swinging their dicks in practically every movie, do you?

Alex stops and faces her.

> ALEX
> Breasts are more acceptable on the screen.

> CHELSEA
> Says who? Men?

A car pulls up and parks nearby.

Chayne exits the car and heads toward the theater. She spots Alex.

CHAYNE
Alex!

Alex and Chelsea turn toward Chayne.

Chayne approaches. She kisses Alex' cheek, very close to his mouth. She is slightly reserved with Chelsea.

ALEX
Chayne, you remember Chelsea?

CHAYNE
Of course.

She flashes Chelsea a dazzling smile.

Chelsea forces a smile.

CHELSEA
Hi. Nice to see you again.

Chayne ignores Chelsea.

CHAYNE
Want to go to dinner later?

Alex nods toward Chelsea.

ALEX
We've already made plans.

CHAYNE
Oh come on, it's been ages.

Alex and Chelsea exchange a glance.

ALEX
Chelsea's at UT in San Antonio and we only see each other on
weekends. Perhaps some other time?

CHAYNE
How about Monday -- lunch?

ALEX
Call me.

Chayne squeezes his hand and hurries toward the theater.

Alex and Chelsea stare after Chayne.

CHELSEA
Is she for real, or what?

They resume walking.

ALEX
She's different, that's for sure.

CHELSEA
Rude little bitch.

Chelsea turns and sends daggers after Chayne.

INT. ALEX' OFFICE - DAY - LATE 1980s

Alex charts stocks on his desktop computer in his cramped office.

His framed undergraduate diploma hangs on the wall and a photo of him with Chelsea and Phillip sits on his desk.

Phone rings.

ALEX
Yes?

SECRETARY
Chayne Evander is here to see you.

Alex frowns.

ALEX
Send her back.

Alex poses, impatient.

Chayne struts into the office and slides into a chair.

CHAYNE
So this is your official place of employment?

ALEX
That was pretty rude of you last weekend.

Chayne peruses the contents of Alex' desk. She picks up the photograph and stares at it.

CHAYNE
What are you doing with that girl, anyway?

> ALEX
> Chelsea is a very good friend, and that's beside the point.

> CHAYNE
> I'm sure all's well. Free for lunch?

Chayne replaces the photograph on the desk.

> ALEX
> It'll cost you.

Chayne, provocative...

> CHAYNE
> I'm buying.

Alex smiles and stands. They exit his office and walk through the secretarial area.

INT. SECRETARIAL AREA - DAY - LATE 1980s

TWO SECRETARIES whisper at a desk.

Alex and Chayne pass.

> ALEX
> See you gorgeous things later.

They watch him pass.

> SECRETARY #1
> He's such a hunk.

> SECRETARY #2

Is that his girlfriend?

They gaze after Alex.

SECRETARY #1
No, Chelsea's the one in the picture on his desk.

They giggle.

INT. RESTAURANT - DAY - LATE 1980s

Chayne and Alex drink wine.

A WAITER clears the table.

CHAYNE
Why don't you look for a place Uptown, close to work?

ALEX
Phillip and I were just looking at the map.

Chayne toys with her wine glass.

CHAYNE
Parting is such sweet sorrow, but once it's done, you're free of the dead weight.

ALEX
And you're available to console me, right?

Chayne smiles widely.

CHAYNE
I'd be lying if I denied that.

INT. CHAYNE'S APARTMENT - DAY - LATE 1980s

Chayne and Alex enter the plush apartment.

Within moments, they slam into a heavy embrace and kiss.

Chayne peels off Alex' jacket, loosens his tie and rips Alex' shirt open.

Buttons fly.

Alex reciprocates. They maul each other stumbling to the sofa where they fall in a passionate embrace.

INT. ALEX AND PHILLIP'S APARTMENT - DAY

Doorbell rings.

Phillip, shirtless, barefoot, in sweat pants, answers the door, grasping an open text book.

David, pie in hand, smiles.

DAVID
Hello neighbor, I'm entering this recipe in a bake-off. Want to be the judge?

Phillip smiles as he steps aside.

David enters the apartment.

PHILLIP
What kind of pie is this?

David runs his hand over Phillip's abs.

DAVID
Sweet and tart strawberry rhubarb.

Phillip gently touches David at the waist. They kiss lightly - a tantalizing sample.

Phillip takes the pie and puts it on an end table.

> PHILLIP
> That's better.

David hooks his thumbs into Phillip's sweat pants at the waist and slowly lowers them as his fingers slide down Phillip's hips.

Phillip smolders.

David kisses Phillip's shin.

> DAVID
> THAT'S better.

INT. ALEX' OFFICE - LATE 1980s

SUPER: TWO WEEKS LATER

Alex sips coffee and stares at the computer monitor. Phone rings.

> ALEX
> Alex.

> CHAYNE (V.O.)
> I found just the place for you.

EXT. ALEX AND PHILLIP'S APARTMENT - DAY - LATE 1980s

A moving truck sits at the curb.

Alex, Phillip, David, Chelsea, and Donna carry down Alex' boxes and furniture.

INT. NEW APARTMENT - NIGHT - LATE 1980s

Alex unpacks boxes.

Chayne sets the table for two and lights candles.

> CHAYNE
> Dinner's ready. Get cleaned up.

INT. ALEX' OFFICE - DAY - LATE 1980s

Alex keys information into the computer.

LOLA enters his office, vase of roses in hand.

> LOLA
> Looks like you've made someone happy.

She sets the vase on the desk.

> ALEX
> Think I'll get a commission?

She laughs and exits.

Alex reaches for the card, reads it and scowls. Phone rings.

> ALEX
> Alex.

> CHAYNE (V.O.)
> Happy anniversary, darling.

Alex turns his chair away from the door. He frowns.

ALEX
We need to talk about this...

INT. GAY NIGHTCLUB - NIGHT - LATE 1980s

Alex and Phillip mingle with PEOPLE.

Alex appears very uncomfortable as Phillip treats Alex as a trophy.

Alex corners Phillip.

ALEX
Let's leave.

Phillip appears perplexed.

PHILLIP
We just got here.

ALEX
What if I see someone I know?

PHILLIP
Don't you think it's time you came out?

ALEX
I don't want you hanging all over me in public.

Phillip pulls back in a huff.

PHILLIP

Maybe you'd better go home and hide.

Alex steps toward Phillip.

> ALEX
> Listen, it's okay when we're alone, but I have a career.
> Friends.

> PHILLIP
> You don't have me.

Phillip turns to leave.

> ALEX
> Perhaps my moving was for the best.

Phillip storms away.

Alex glances around, uncomfortable, notices an exit and heads toward it, brushing interested MEN aside.

INT. ALEX' APARTMENT - NIGHT - LATE 1980s

Alex lies in bed.

Boxes stand in the shadows, waiting to be unpacked.

He stares at the ceiling, his face clouded with emotion. He reaches for the phone and dials.

> ALEX
> Did I wake you?

INT. CHELSEA'S APARTMENT - SAN ANTONIO - NIGHT - LATE 1980s

Alex and Chelsea lie in bed, under the tangled covers, in a tender embrace.

CHELSEA
That was incredible.

Alex nuzzles her neck.

ALEX
There's so much more where that came from.

Chelsea tenderly holds his face and kisses him.

CHELSEA
Three times in one night?

ALEX
It's almost another day.

They melt together in a kiss; Chelsea throws her legs around his waist, they rock to the rhythm of love making.

INT. RESTAURANT - DAY - LATE 1980s

Alex and Phillip relax over a glass of wine.

ALEX
How's David?

PHILLIP
His catering business has taken off. He has to turn clients away.

ALEX
That's good. When there's a demand, he can pick and choose.

PHILLIP
Want to take in a movie tonight?

ALEX
Can't. Chelsea's up for the weekend and we're going to a dinner party at her folks place.

Phillip takes an aggressive stance.

PHILLIP
Chelsea, Chelsea, Chelsea. What the hell's going on with you lately?

Alex squirms.

ALEX
What do you mean?

PHILLIP
Every time I call, you're busy with Chelsea. Is this a... relationship?

Alex pulls a deep sigh.

ALEX
Yes.

Phillip flinches.

PHILLIP
Who do you think you're kidding?

ALEX

I need more in a relationship... an acceptable...

PHILLIP
You just don't want anyone to know you're gay.

ALEX
Bi. I'm not gay; I have bisexual tendencies, same as you.

PHILLIP
I am not bi. I'm gay.

ALEX
Well I'm not when I'm wrapped in the arms of a beautiful
woman like Chelsea.

PHILLIP
I'd advise you to look inside your closet, man.

Phillip shoves his chair back and exits abruptly.

Alex smiles weakly at PEOPLE nearby.

INT. ALEX' NEW OFFICE - DAY - 1990s

SUPER: FOUR YEARS LATER

Alex sits at a large desk in his spacious new office.

A framed photo of Chelsea adorns a corner of his desk, along
with the older photo.

Two diplomas hang on the wall.

He toys with a jewelers ring box. Lola enters.

ALEX

Reservations?

LOLA
Check.

ALEX
Flowers?

LOLA
Check.
(beat)
Ring?

Alex lifts the box.

ALEX
Check. Think she'll have me?

LOLA
Double check.

EXT. CHELSEA'S NEW APARTMENT - HOUSTON - NIGHT - 1990s

Alex stands at the door with a floral box in hand. He rings the doorbell.

Chelsea, dressed for dinner, opens the door and is surprised as Alex hands her the box.

CHELSEA
Flowers?

ALEX

Flowers for a beautiful woman.

Chelsea holds the door open and Alex enters.

INT. UPSCALE RESTAURANT - NIGHT - 1990s

Alex and Chelsea sit in a dimly lit cozy corner, a bucket of wine beside their table.

CHELSEA
You must have had quite a day trading.

ALEX
Wouldn't trade this day for the world.

CHELSEA
So tell me the good news. Did you get a promotion?

ALEX
No, but I need to ask you a question.

CHELSEA
What?

ALEX
Will you marry me?

Chelsea appears blown away.

CHELSEA
Are you serious?

ALEX
Flowers, reservations, wine...

He pulls the box from his jacket pocket, opens and pushes it across the table to Chelsea.

ALEX
Ring.

Chelsea picks up the box and stares at the huge diamond. She glances toward Alex.

CHELSEA
This is beautiful Alex.

She lifts the ring out of the box.

ALEX
Let me.

Alex takes the ring and slips it on her finger.

He kisses her fingers.

Chelsea admires the ring.

ALEX
What do you say?

Chelsea leans forward, grasps his hand and gazes deep into his eyes.

CHELSEA
It fits.

Both beam.

INT. CHELSEA AND ALEX' NEW APARTMENT - AFTERNOON - 1990s

Chelsea, Alex, Phillip and Donna admire a table of wedding gifts.

ALEX
I should have gotten married years ago. Look at all this loot.

DONNA
I can't wait to see what you haul in at the wedding.

Phillip stares hard at Alex.

They all drift to the living room.

DONNA
You sure have the place fixed up nice.

ALEX
The official domicile next weekend.

PHILLIP
Wait 'til he dumps a wet towel on the shoes you're planning to wear to work.

All eyes rivet to Alex.

ALEX
I was a slovenly college student.

CHELSEA
I thought you each had your own bathrooms and closets.

> DONNA
> My brothers are slobs.

> ALEX
> Guys borrow things just like girls do.

Phillip vents.

> PHILLIP
> Yeah, and he never cleans the kitchen after cooking.

Alex simmers.

> ALEX
> Yes I do.

Chelsea and Donna watch the exchange.

Phillip bitterly bickers.

> PHILLIP
> No you didn't. You've always had someone else to pick up
> after you.

> ALEX
> You make me sound like an untrained dog.

> PHILLIP
> Good metaphor. Don't forget which way to mount next week.

Phillip abruptly stands.

> PHILLIP

I told David I'd pick up some things... I'd better go.

ALEX
I'll walk you out.

Alex stands abruptly and they exit.

Chelsea and Donna are perplexed.

DONNA
Is Phillip jealous?

CHELSEA
He's never ever made a pass at me and he's had plenty of
opportunity.

They go to a window and watch.

EXT. APARTMENT COMPLEX - AFTERNOON - 1990s

Phillip huffs to his car, Alex in pursuit. He unlocks the car and
Alex grabs his arm before he can get the door open.

ALEX
Just what the hell was that all about?

Phillip controls his rage.

PHILLIP
I can't believe you're going through with this charade.

ALEX
I love Chelsea.

PHILLIP
Do you love her more than me?

ALEX
Phillip, I'll always love you. This is different...

PHILLIP
Different?

ALEX
I want a normal life... a family... kids, is that too much to ask for?

PHILLIP
Normal? You're as queer as a three dollar bill.

Now it's Alex' turn to control rage.

ALEX
You're just angry because I'll be sleeping with someone else.

PHILLIP
What else is new? You could never be faithful to anyone.

ALEX
That's not true.

PHILLIP
How can you stand there and argue when you've had dozens of male lovers and Chelsea is the only woman you've ever been with?

ALEX

There have been others. You just didn't know about them.

Shocked, Phillip yanks the car door open and gets in.

Alex closes the door for him, with force.

> ALEX
> You really hate to see me happy with someone else, don't you?

Phillip starts the car.

> PHILLIP
> You're getting into something that will never stay together.

> ALEX
> People change, you know. I've changed.

Phillip spins out of the parking lot.

Alex watches him leave, then returns to the apartment.

INT. ALEX AND CHELSEA'S APARTMENT - DAY

Alex returns and sits, smoldering.

> DONNA
> What was that all about?

> ALEX
> He's just jealous that he doesn't have someone.

> CHELSEA
> He could have had Donna.

> DONNA

Oh please. Phillip and I were real good friends, but I'll tell
you...

Donna leans forward.

DONNA
He's impotent.

Alex appears amazed.

CHELSEA
You're kidding?

ALEX
Maybe you two just didn't have the right chemistry.

DONNA
Couldn't keep it up, and he's got enough to keep up, too.

Chelsea gapes at Donna.

CHELSEA
Girl, you are wicked.

Alex shakes his head.

ALEX
And they say men talk...

Chelsea and Donna giggle.

INT. CHURCH - DAY - 1990s

The church is packed with FRIENDS and RELATIVES as Chelsea and Alex are married by a PRIEST.

Donna, elated as the maid of honor, is flanked by six BRIDESMAIDS.

Phillip, stone-faced, is best man flanked by six USHERS.

Alex and Chelsea's father's beam.

Their mothers dab their eyes with tissue.

INT. COUNTRY CLUB - RECEPTION - DAY - 1990s

The place is decked out with wedding finery.

David, in a tux-type chefs coat shows off the magnificent five-tier wedding cake as GUESTS mingle.

He shoots off directions to his STAFF AD LIB.

Alex and Chelsea appear radiant.

Donna, happy as a lark, is paired off with Phillip.

Phillip appears distracted.

Chelsea and Alex make their way over to David.

Chelsea grabs David in a tremendous hug.

CHELSEA
David... this is all so wonderful! You're fantastic.

DAVID
I wanted it to be perfect for you, Chelsea.

Chelsea and David kiss lightly.

ALEX
Hey.

DAVID
She loves me for my food.

EXT. CEMETERY - CURRENT DAY

A soft breeze comes up and ruffles the flowers on the coffin as the Priest continues the ceremony.

Chelsea kisses Janie on the top of her head as she stares straight ahead.

Jason leans against Alex. Alex bends and picks him up. He holds him tightly as he squeezes his eyes shut in anguish.

INT. ALEX AND CHELSEA'S APARTMENT - DAY - 1990s

Chelsea, rounded with pregnancy, plops down on the sofa beside Alex, bag of pretzels in hand.

He rubs her stomach, leans over and kisses it.

ALEX
Mommy is being bad but daddy is watching out for you.

She clunks him with the bag then offers him the bag.

ALEX
Watch your salt intake.

Chelsea points to the label: salt free.

ALEX

Let me see those.

He grabs the bag, pulls out a handful and pops one in his mouth. He makes a face.

                    ALEX
                Cardboard.

Chelsea gets up and goes to the kitchen.

                  CHELSEA
               Want a drink?

Alex, stone-faced, stares ahead.

                    ALEX
                  Sure.

He reaches for the phone and dials.

                    ALEX
            Hey! Get unpacked?

Chelsea returns and sits.

                    ALEX
                Need help?

Chelsea questions with her eyes.

Alex kisses Chelsea on the cheek.

                    ALEX

Phillip says hi.

He holds the phone away from his ear so Chelsea can hear furniture being scraped across wood floors.

> ALEX
> You're going to ruin the floor.
> (beat)
> Listen, give me a minute and I'll help.

Chelsea giggles. Alex hangs up.

> CHELSEA
> What was he pushing?

Alex stands.

> ALEX
> That big armoire. Be back in a couple of hours.

Chelsea gets comfortable.

> CHELSEA
> Have fun.

INT. PHILLIP'S APARTMENT - DAY - 1990s

Phillip, in sweat pants only, moves boxes. Doorbell rings.

He opens the door and Alex enters. They embrace heavily.

> PHILLIP
> You alright?

They part.

> ALEX
>
> I cannot make love to her anymore.

> PHILLIP
>
> Isn't that kind of normal?

They flop on the sofa.

> ALEX
>
> You don't understand what I mean...

Phillip appears clueless.

> PHILLIP
>
> Lost your sex drive?

Alex reaches for Phillip and pulls him into an embrace.

> ALEX
>
> I thought so...

They kiss passionately.

INT. DELIVERY ROOM - NIGHT - 1990s

Chelsea bears down.

Alex sits beside her, masked and in hospital greens, coaching.

> ALEX
>
> Push!

Chelsea screams as she bears down.

> **CHELSEA**
> Is the baby okay?

The DOCTOR and NURSES perform their duties.

> **DOCTOR**
> Little bit more. Baby's fine.

Chelsea and Alex breathe together. He grips her hand.

> **ALEX**
> Okay, deep breath. Push!

Chelsea bears down. She wrenches his hand.

Alex grimaces.

> **DOCTOR**
> Your son thinks you did a good job.

The Doctor holds up JASON.

Alex and Chelsea are deliriously happy.

INT. HOSPITAL - NIGHT - 1990s

Alex stands outside the nursery with his parents, Phillip, David, Donna and Chelsea's parents. He smiles proudly.

Phillip, David and Donna wave at Jason. Chelsea's father slaps Alex on the back.

Chelsea's mother hooks her arm through Alex' mother's arm.

Alex stares in wonder at Jason.

INT. JASON'S ROOM - NIGHT - 1990s

SUPER: ONE MONTH LATER

In the glow of the night light, Alex cradles Jason in his arms and sways gently.

ALEX
...and daddy will build you a sandbox.

He smiles down at Jason.

Jason smiles.

Alex kisses Jason.

ALEX
You're so beautiful. I can't believe Mommy and I made such a perfect thing.

Jason yawns and closes his eyes.

Alex sways a moment longer, then gently lays Jason in the crib. He watches over him a moment, then quietly exits.

INT. MASTER BEDROOM - NIGHT - 1990s

Chelsea lays wide awake as Alex enters the room.

CHELSEA
Was he wet?

Alex gets into bed.

ALEX

I think he just wanted company.

He turns off the light.

Chelsea reaches for him.

They turn to each other and kiss lightly.

ALEX
Aren't we supposed to wait a couple more weeks?

Chelsea pulls him closer and kisses him deeper.

She reaches under her pillow and pulls out a condom and waves it at him.

Alex pulls away.

ALEX
I think we should wait. I don't want to hurt you.

Chelsea turns on her back in a huff.

CHELSEA
It's been months.

ALEX
Then what's a couple more weeks? One more trip to the doctor for the official okay.

Chelsea turns her back on Alex, angry.

CHELSEA
Since when were you ever interested in what the doctor had to say?

Alex lays in bed and stares at the ceiling.

He rolls into her and pulls her close.

He buries his face in her hair.

Jason cries O.S.

Alex gets up and goes to him.

> ALEX (O.S.)
> Chelsea!

Chelsea springs out of bed.

INT. ALEX AND CHELSEA'S APARTMENT - DAY - 1990s

SUPER: 6 MONTHS LATER

Chelsea feeds Jason, six months old, while she cradles the phone.

> CHELSEA
> Mom, Jason will be fine, he has a bronchial condition. It's not life threatening. We found a nice French lady with impeccable references. Maybe she'll teach him French.

Jason finishes eating. Chelsea wipes his face.

> CHELSEA
> I can't wait to get back to work. I love my job.

INT. ALEX' OFFICE - DAY - 1990s

Alex concentrates on the computer monitor. A corner of his desk is crowded with pictures of Jason.

ANDREA, 28, another stock broker, poses in the doorway.

> ANDREA
> Any plans for lunch?

Alex leans back in the chair and smiles.

> ALEX
> I'm tied up right now. Can I take a rain check?

Andrea slinks into the office and slides into a chair.

> ANDREA
> Then I'm just the person you need. I have Girl Scout badges in knot tying.

Alex appears perplexed.

> ALEX
> We'd better check out those skills. You might be rusty.

He gets up, walks around the side of the desk and helps her to her feet. They exit.

INT. ALEX AND CHELSEA'S APARTMENT - NIGHT - 1990s

The front door creeps open and Alex tip-toes into the dark apartment.

He takes off his shoes by the front door and loosens and removes his tie as he heads for the bedroom.

He steps on a baby rattler, grimaces, picks it up and hangs his head.

He enters the bedroom, undresses and slides into bed.

Chelsea sleeps on her side. Her eyes open, she squeezes them shut as a tear escapes.

INT. CHELSEA'S OFFICE - DAY - 1990s

Chelsea, in a white doctor's coat, enters an examining room. She approaches her PATIENT.

> PATIENT
> Welcome back. How's motherhood?

> CHELSEA
> Wonderful.

Chelsea picks up a photo book from the counter and opens it.

The photo's cascade, accordion-like.

The Patient laughs.

INT. ALEX AND CHELSEA'S KITCHEN - AFTER-NOON - 1990s

Chelsea prepares a salad.

Jason, ten months old, in a walker, clutches her legs in tears. Water boils on the stove.

O.S. the front door shuts.

> ALEX (O.S.)
> I'm home!

Alex enters the kitchen and picks up Jason.

ALEX
What's all the fuss?

He turns to Chelsea and gives her a peck on the cheek.

Chelsea turns slightly and sniffs his collar.

CHELSEA
Work late again?

Alex goes to a cabinet, grabs plates and sets them on the table.

Chelsea scrutinizes Alex.

ALEX
Working on the Donnaly account.

He gets silverware and napkins and finishes setting the table.

CHELSEA
You'd better suggest to Fred Donnaly not to use his wife's
perfume then.

She turns back to the counter and forcefully chops
vegetables.

Alex sits and bounces Jason on his legs.

ALEX
Fred Donnaly can wear anything he wants. He just turned over
a quarter of a million dollars for me to invest.

CHELSEA
Really?

Chelsea slams the knife down on the counter, grabs Jason and exits the kitchen in a huff.

Alex appears dismayed. He gets up, turns off the stove and pursues Chelsea to Jason's room.

INT. JASON'S ROOM - 1990s

Chelsea changes Jason. Alex leans on the doorjamb.

> ALEX
>
> I'm sorry I got in so late last night. I told you I was going to be working late.

Chelsea turns to face Alex.

> CHELSEA
>
> Cut the bullshit, Alex. You've been late three times this week and smelled like a French whorehouse when you came home.

They stare each other down.

Jason plays with his toes.

Chelsea turns back to Jason.

> CHELSEA
>
> If fatherhood is too much for you, just say so.

Alex rakes his hair.

> ALEX
>
> Where did that idea came from? I love you and Jason.

Chelsea completes the change, picks up Jason and kisses him.

CHELSEA

While you were out "working" we were at the emergency room.

Chelsea brushes past Alex.

ALEX

Why the hell didn't you call me?

Alex pursues her.

CHELSEA

I did Alex. I called the office, your cell phone, and pager. I even emailed you!

ALEX

Chelsea! Let's talk this through.

INT. ALEX AND CHELSEA'S KITCHEN - AFTER-NOON - 1990s

Alex enters the kitchen.

Chelsea is at the stove.

Jason in his walker eating a cracker.

CHELSEA

I'm going to go stay with my folks for a while.

Alex appears stunned.

ALEX

Is that necessary?

CHELSEA

I wouldn't have brought it up if I didn't think it was.

Alex sits abruptly.

INT. ALEX' OFFICE - DAY - 1990s

Alex chats with Phillip.

PHILLIP

Is this postpartum blues?

Alex shrugs.

ALEX

She's been very sensitive about me working late.

Andrea sticks her head in the office, not noticing Phillip.

ANDREA

Good morning, Tiger.

Alex frowns as he avoids Andrea's seductive glance and faces off with Phillip.

Andrea turns and notices Phillip.

ANDREA

Oh, I didn't know you had company.

Phillip smolders intense rage. He gets up and extends a hand.

PHILLIP

Hi, I'm Jason's God Father.

Andrea, in tight control, takes his hand.

> ANDREA
> Hi. Nice to meet you.

She glances at her watch.

> ANDREA
> Gosh, I've got to get to a meeting.
> (to Phillip)
> Sorry, have to run.
> (to Alex)
> A meeting.

She hurries off.

Phillip and Alex glare at each other.

Alex gets up and closes the door. He faces Phillip.

> ALEX
> I can explain...

> PHILLIP
> You'll fuck anything with legs.

Alex returns to his chair.

> ALEX
> Oh, like you're so innocent?

> PHILLIP
> I don't have a wife and a sick child.

ALEX

So, it's okay as long as it's you?

Phillip stands.

PHILLIP

You're a slut.

Phillip storms out of the office.

The Secretaries eyes follow him out the door.

Alex releases a deep breath.

INT. ALEX AND CHELSEA'S APARTMENT - AFTER-
NOON - 1990s

Alex opens the door and enters.

ALEX

I'm home!

INTERCUT AS NEEDED

He walks to the spotless kitchen and stands in the doorway for a moment. Then he retraces his steps and veers off to the bedrooms.

He enters Jason's room and glances around, backs out and heads to the master bedroom.

ALEX

Chelsea?

Alex opens Chelsea's closet to find a huge gap of missing clothes. He opens a bureau drawer to find it empty.

He sits on the edge of the bed and slumps down, head in hands.

INT. ALEX AND CHELSEA'S APARTMENT - NIGHT - 1990s

Alex sits by the phone in the darkened living room illuminated by a small reading lamp. He picks up the phone and dials.

> ALEX
> Hello, is Chelsea there?
> (beat)
> Can I talk to her?

He closes his eyes in pain.

> ALEX
> I see. Well tell her I called.

He hangs up the phone quietly and stares into space. He picks up the phone and dials again.

> ALEX
> Mom? Mom, I made a huge mistake...

Alex cries softly.

INT. ALEX AND CHELSEA'S APARTMENT - DAY - 1990s

Alex enters the apartment, briefcase in hand.

Chelsea rises from the sofa.

Alex is cautiously happy.

> ALEX

Chelsea, I...

Chelsea explodes.

CHELSEA
I asked Lola about the Donnaly account. She told me about
that little barracuda, Andrea. How she was after you.

ALEX
Lola didn't have any business...

CHELSEA
You'll just lie right through to the end, won't you?

ALEX
I never lied to you, Chelsea.

CHELSEA
You betrayed me Alex. You turned to another woman and then
came home to me in the middle of the night. What if she has
AIDS?

ALEX
AIDS? Chelsea, Andrea does not have AIDS.

CHELSEA
You know everyone else she's slept with and who they've slept
with?

ALEX
It was a mistake. One mistake.

CHELSEA

So what are you going to do now, Alex?

ALEX

It's over. It was a fling and I'll never see her again.

CHELSEA

Does that mean you're going to look for another job?

ALEX

If I have to... if she doesn't leave the firm, I will.

CHELSEA

The alternative is to find a lawyer because I'm not going to accept anything less. Jason and I come first in your life. Never second.

Chelsea storms out the door, slamming it in her wake.

INT. ALEX AND CHELSEA'S APARTMENT - DAY - 1990s

SUPER: ONE MONTH LATER

Alex, in shorts enters the messy kitchen.

He stands in the doorway and looks around as if seeing the mess for the first time.

He approaches the counter and begins to gather up the clutter and clean.

INT. LIVING ROOM - NIGHT - 1990s

Alex slouches in a chair, phone in hand. He stares at separate pictures of Chelsea and Jason.

His eyes rest on a photo of Phillip.

ALEX

Chelsea, I promise I'll never touch another woman as long as I live. Please, come back home.

He listens.

ALEX

I promise.

CHELSEA (V.O.)

Alex was true to his word; he never looked at another woman.

Alex hangs up the phone. Doorbell rings.

Phillip enters. He and Alex embrace and walk somberly to the sofa.

INT. ALEX AND CHELSEA'S APARTMENT - DAY - 1990s

A football game fills the room as Alex stares blankly at the TV screen.

A key turns in the lock at the front door.

Alex turns toward the door, disbelief on his face as Chelsea enters, Jason in her arms and diaper bag in tow.

Alex mutes the TV and awkwardly approaches Chelsea. He hugs them in a tight embrace as tears run down his face.

ALEX

I'm sorry Chelsea. I love you and Jason so much.

Chelsea breaks down and cries.

INT. ALEX' OFFICE - DAY - 1990s

SUPER: ONE YEAR LATER

Alex is on the phone.

Lola enters and puts a piece of paper in front of him.

ALEX

The presentation is tomorrow at 2:00. We're flying in tonight.
It's all arranged. I'll see you tomorrow.

He hangs up the phone.

LOLA

Here's your plane ticket and itinerary. I've got tickets for you
and Phillip to see Cats.

Alex stands and kisses her cheek.

ALEX

You are a wondrous woman.

He grabs his jacket and slips into it.

LOLA

See you in a couple of days.

ALEX

I'm out of here.

He exits.

INT. ALEX AND CHELSEA'S NEW TOWNHOUSE -
DAY - 1990s

Chelsea, four months pregnant, packs a small bag.

Alex exits the closet, two ties in hand.

ALEX

Which do you think I should wear for the presentation?

Chelsea takes and studies both ties and heads for the closet.

CHELSEA

I think this one for the presentation and this one for anything else.

She hands him two different ties.

Alex kisses her.

ALEX

You're so right. What would I do without you?

He holds her tenderly.

CHELSEA

Phillip should be here any second.

Doorbell rings.

ALEX

Speak of the devil and he shall come.

O.S. door opens.

PHILLIP (O.S.)

You ready?

Phillip enters the bedroom.

                    CHELSEA
                  Almost there.

Phillip kisses Chelsea's cheek.

                    PHILLIP
           How's my favorite wife-person.

                    CHELSEA
                   Still sick.

                    PHILLIP
         You're still having morning sickness?

                     ALEX
                 Like clockwork.

Chelsea closes the suitcase and turns to the suit bag. She takes
mental inventory then zips it up.

                    CHELSEA
              Okay. You're ready to sail.

Alex grabs the suit bag.

Phillip grabs the suitcase.

                     ALEX
               I'll call you tonight.

He kisses her and they exit the room.

Alex and Phillip peek in on Jason, asleep in his crib, then leave.

INT. HOTEL BAR - NIGHT - 1990s

Alex and Phillip toy with drinks at the bar, a basket of pretzels in front of them.

CHUCK, not quite 40, laid-back, and TIM, over 40, take the next two barstools and order drinks.

Chuck leans close to Alex.

> ### CHUCK
> Can I steal a pretzel?

Alex appraises Chuck and smiles coolly. He passes the basket.

> ### ALEX
> Can't stand to see a man go hungry.

Chuck smiles and grabs a pretzel. He bites it with zeal as he stares intently at Alex.

> ### CHUCK
> I'm starving.

He brushes off his hand and extends it to Alex.

> ### CHUCK
> Chuck.

Alex grasps his hand.

> ### ALEX
> Alex. Investments. And you... let me guess.

Alex surveys Chuck with a leisurely once-over.

ALEX
Geologist?

CHUCK
Close. Doctor. Both dig for clues, don't they?

They share a laugh.

The four strike up a conversation AD LIB.

LATER

The four sit at a table and laugh and talk AD LIB.

Alex gets up and stretches.

ALEX
Think I'll call it a night.

Chuck stands.

CHUCK
Same here.

Phillip and Tim remain seated.

PHILLIP
It's early!

Phillip and Tim laugh.

Alex and Chuck walk toward the elevator.

INT. LIVING ROOM - DAY - 1990s

Chelsea, very pregnant, paces the floor, hands on lower back.

Alex rushes into the room with an overnight bag.

Doorbell rings.

Phillip enters, gym bag in hand. He drops it on the floor.

                    PHILLIP
                Where's my big boy?

Jason, two years old, gallops into the living room and grabs
Phillip's legs and squeals.

Phillip hoists Jason in the air and plays with him.

                    CHELSEA
            You sure you'll be okay with this?

                    PHILLIP
        No, guess you'd better cancel the trip to the hospital.

                    CHELSEA
    I left Jason's medicine on the kitchen counter in case he gets
                    congested.

                    PHILLIP
                We'll cough together.

Alex, tense as a corkscrew, checks and rechecks the bag.

                    ALEX
        Brush, moisturizer, robe, nightgown...

He rushes from the room and returns with another piece of clothing and stuffs it into the bag.

CHELSEA
Enough. Let's get going.

Phillip swings Jason onto his hip and walks them to the door.

PHILLIP
Maybe you'd better let Chelsea drive.

Alex smiles tightly.

ALEX
You've never done this before, remember?

PHILLIP
I was here the first time.

Chelsea kisses Jason on the cheek, then Phillip.

CHELSEA
Be nice to Uncle Phillip.

Jason waves as Alex and Chelsea exit and Phillip stands in the doorway.

Phillip closes the door.

PHILLIP
Let's see what trouble we can get into, okay?

Phillip puts Jason down.

Jason claps and shrieks as he runs off toward his room.

Phillip follows.

INT. HOSPITAL - DAY - 1990s

Chelsea lays in bed with JANIE, all cleaned up, cradled in her arms.

Alex sits on the edge of the bed, rubbing Janie's hands with a finger.

> ALEX
> God, we make beautiful babies.

Chelsea smiles and covers Alex' hand with hers. They both gaze adoringly at Janie.

Both sets of grandparents enter the room bearing flowers and gifts.

Alex' Father hands him a box of cigars.

INT. ALEX AND CHELSEA'S TOWNHOUSE - DAY - 1990s

Chelsea and Alex' Mothers help out with the kids.

Chelsea lies on the couch reading to Jason while her mom feeds Janie a bottle.

> CHELSEA'S MOM
> It's a shame Phillip came down with the flu.

Alex enters the room with a glass for Chelsea. He puts it on the end table near her.

ALEX
Bronchitis. His whole family gets it all the time.

Alex' mom enters from the kitchen.

ALEX' MOM
Didn't Phillip have asthma in high school?

ALEX
Yeah, he and his kid brother wheezed continuously.

CHELSEA
And we've got our own little wheezer right here.

ALEX' MOM
Let's hope Janie doesn't follow suit.

INT. DOCTOR ADAMS OFFICE - DAY - 1990s

Phillip sits on an examining table fully clothed. The door opens and DOCTOR ADAMS enters.

DOCTOR ADAMS
Still haven't moved to Arizona, huh?

Phillip wheezes a laugh.

DOCTOR ADAMS
That doesn't sound good.

He takes the stethoscope and listens to Phillip's chest, then his back.

DOCTOR ADAMS
Lots of rattling in there.

He presses the glands on the side of his neck and notices a spot.

He lifts the hair off the back of Phillip's neck and a nickel sized spot appears.

DOCTOR ADAMS
Phillip, we need to have a serious talk.

Doctor Adams sits and faces Phillip.

LATER

A NURSE, in gloves, draws blood from Phillip's arm. She places a cotton ball on his arm.

NURSE
Hold your arm up for a few minutes. Want a band-aid?

Phillip follows orders.

PHILLIP
I'd rather be jabbed again than pull a band-aid off.

They share a laugh.

NURSE
Doctor Adams will be back in a few minutes.

The nurse exits.

Phillip gets up and paces. He checks out his arm and throws the cotton away.

PHILLIP
Jesus. Jesus Christ.

Doctor Adams enters, grim faced.

Phillip sits on the examining table.

Doctor Adams takes the stool and rolls in front of Phillip.

DOCTOR ADAMS
AIDS tests are pretty sophisticated now, not like they were ten years ago. We'll have the results back in a jiffy, and I'll personally call you.

Phillip visually slumps.

DOCTOR ADAMS
I'm going to give you something for the pneumonia. It's just a slight case but we've got to monitor it real close. Don't want any complications to set in.

PHILLIP
What do you think?

Doctor Adams pats Phillip's arm.

DOCTOR ADAMS
This is not a guessing game, Phillip. I'd say there's a very high possibility that the test will come back positive.

INT. ALEX' OFFICE - DAY - 1990s

Alex punches numbers into the keypad on the computer. Phone rings.

ALEX
Alex.

He springs to life.

ALEX
Chuck! How's the doctor business these days?
(beat)
Listen, Chelsea and I are throwing a little dinner party
Saturday night. Think you can make it? Great.

Alex disconnects and dials.

ALEX
Is my beautiful wife drilling, or is she free?
(beat)
I just invited someone to the party. I promise -- no one else.
Chuck. Great guy, doctor, met him on the trip to New York.
Love you. Go drill for gold.

He hangs up and smiles.

INT. ALEX AND CHELSEA'S TOWNHOUSE - NIGHT - 1990s

Chelsea and David man the kitchen.

INT. LIVING ROOM - NIGHT - 1990s

Alex, Donna, Lola and GUESTS drink wine, mingle and chat.

INT. DINING ROOM - NIGHT - 1990s

The table is set elegantly with china, crystal, a gorgeous floral centerpiece, and several lit candles.

Doorbell rings. Alex gets the door.

Chuck enters, exotic flowers in hand. They embrace for just a little too long.

> ALEX
> Gorgeous flowers. Chelsea will love them.

Chuck leans forward and whispers.

> CHUCK
> I remembered the flowers in the room.

Alex steers Chuck toward the kitchen.

> ALEX
> Behave. I'll introduce you.

They push through to the kitchen.

INT. KITCHEN - NIGHT - 1990s

Alex and Chuck come into the kitchen.

> ALEX
> Hon. This is Chuck Winsome, the doctor I met at the seminar in New York.

Chelsea turns around and gasps at the flowers.

> CHELSEA
> Oh, how beautiful.

She wipes her hands on a dishtowel then takes the flowers from Chuck and smells them.

> CHELSEA
>
> You shouldn't have, but I'm glad you did. How nice to meet you.

> CHUCK
>
> Beauty deserves beautiful things.

He kisses her cheek.

> CHELSEA
>
> (to Alex)
>
> Give him anything he wants.

She kisses both on the cheek.

Alex and Chuck smile knowingly as they make eye contact.

> CHELSEA
>
> Chuck, this is David, a friend of ours who happens to be the best gourmet chef in the entire city.

David and Chuck shake.

> DAVID
>
> You see where all my advertising dollars go?

> CHELSEA
>
> We about ready?

> DAVID

Get them in their chairs.

Alex and Chuck scoot out of the room.

INT. DINING ROOM- NIGHT - 1990s

All are seated as David and Chelsea carry elegantly arranged plates and set them before the diners.

AD LIB enthusiasm from all.

David and Chelsea join the others at the table. Alex raises his glass in a toast.

> ALEX
> To the best cook in Houston.

All partake the wine then dig into the food.

LATER

> DONNA
> Just when I think you could never top the last performance, you do it again.

> CHELSEA
> David should cook for royalty. Too bad Phillip couldn't be here.

Alex has a moment of guilt.

> ALEX
> Wouldn't do him any good -- taste buds are probably dead.

Chuck ignores the subject.

CHUCK

This is the best meal I've ever had and I used to think I couldn't be outdone.

Chuck raises his glass to David.

David beams at all the praise.

DAVID

Wait till you see desert.

He exits into the kitchen and returns with a five-layered mocha cream torte cake.

Groans from around the table.

INT. ALEX AND CHELSEA'S TOWNHOUSE - DAY - HOME GYM - 1990s

Chelsea works the stair-stepper at a brisk pace.

Jason, three years old, raises a one-pound weight over his head.

JASON

Look mommy!

CHELSEA

What a strong, healthy little boy!

Jason beams as he raises the weight over his head with two hands.

He bonks himself on the head and runs crying to Chelsea.

Chelsea quits her workout and smothers him in kisses.

Doorbell rings.

INT. LIVING ROOM - FOYER - DAY - 1990s

A bag of golf clubs stands by the door. Chelsea answers the door.

Chuck enters, small shopping bag in hand.

CHUCK
Hi, darling. Finish your workout?

They peck each other on the cheek.

CHELSEA
Uh-huh. What bribery did you bring this time?

Chuck chuckles lightly.

CHUCK
Bribery?
(in a raised voice)
Pooh Bear brought his honey pot.

Jason squeals with delight and charges up to Chuck.

Chelsea looks on, very pleased.

Alex enters with Janie, one year old, on his hip.

ALEX
What's going on? Did Uncle Chuck bring you something special?

JASON
Pooh Bear!

They make their way to the sofa.

Chuck sits and Jason clambers onto the sofa beside him.

Chelsea and Alex sit opposite.

Chuck removes a stuffed Pooh Bear from the bag, with a honey pot and honey swizzle stick.

Chuck removes the swizzle stick from the pot and turns to Jason.

CHUCK
Let's give this to Mommy to keep so Pooh doesn't lose it, okay?

Jason nods, grabs the swizzle stick from Chuck and dashes over to Chelsea and dumps it in her waiting hand.

CHELSEA
Thank you.

Jason returns to Chuck and sits on the sofa, anxious for the gift.

Chuck hands over the bear.

ALEX
What do you say, Jason?

JASON
Thank you!

Chuck shakes the bag at Janie.

CHUCK
Is something in the bag for Janie?

Janie gets excited and bounces in Alex' lap.

Chelsea laughs.

> CHELSEA
> You're crazy.

Chuck dramatically sticks his hand in the bag and pulls out a brightly colored rubber duck and squeaks it.

Janie screeches excitedly and lunges for the duck.

> ALEX
> Whoa!

All laugh as Chuck hands over the duck to Janie who immediately bites it on the head and smiles big.

Alex kisses her on the head and hands her over to Chelsea.

> ALEX
> Time to let 'em fly.

Chuck and Alex head for the door.

> CHELSEA
> Knock 'em dead.

Chuck turns.

> CHUCK
> I don't want to work today!

They share a laugh.

INT. CHUCK'S HI-RISE - DAY - 1990s

Chuck and Alex' golf clothes are scattered throughout the living room.

EXT. CHUCK'S HI-RISE - DAY - 1990s

Chuck and Alex lounge in a hot tub and drink wine.

> ALEX
> This is what I call playing a round.

Chuck has a momentarily feeling of guilt.

> CHUCK
> I hate sneaking around behind Chelsea's back.

Alex sobers.

> ALEX
> I never should have dragged her into this web.

> CHUCK
> Why did you get married?

> ALEX
> I wanted the American dream... wife, kids, house, dog.

> CHUCK
> Sometimes it's hard to accept who you are.

> ALEX
> I have these two beautiful kids and Chelsea is the best. I
> wouldn't change that for anything.

Chuck refills their glasses.

CHUCK
Yeah, but what are you going to do if she ever finds out?

ALEX
I'll never give her the opportunity to think in that direction. I
had an affair with a woman I worked with...

Chuck appears quite surprised.

ALEX
It was an identity thing. I couldn't run back to Phillip like a yo-
yo.

CHUCK
How long did this last?

ALEX
I only slept with her once. She just didn't interest me.

CHUCK
David really crimped your style, didn't he?

Alex guzzles wine.

ALEX
I don't know what I was thinking or doing. I was addicted to
Phillip. He's been there since high school. I didn't love him, I
used him.

CHUCK
Are you using me?

Alex appears stunned.

                    ALEX
I've never felt so at peace in my life. I have what I want.
                    Do you?

Chuck drinks in Alex.

                    CHUCK
No one could be as lucky as I am. I have you, your beautiful
    children to watch grow up, and a wonderful friend in
                    Chelsea.

They share the moment.

INT. ALEX AND CHELSEA'S TOWNHOUSE - NIGHT -
1990s

Chelsea and Alex get ready for bed.

                    CHELSEA
I'm so glad you've got Chuck for a friend.

Alex' eyes widen in surprise as his back is to her.

                    ALEX
                    Why's that?

                    CHELSEA
You never fight with Chuck like you do with Phillip.

Alex slips into bed and grabs a book off the end table.

                    ALEX

That's because Phillip is possessive and a control freak and
Chuck is sane.

Chelsea brushes her hair.

CHELSEA
It's not that I don't like Phillip -- he's our children's God father.

ALEX
I know what you're trying to say. I'm glad you like Chuck. He
loves you and the kids.

CHELSEA
We love him too.

Chelsea turns off the overhead light and gets in bed. She snuggles with Alex.

He lays the book on his chest and holds her to him, his expression blank.

INT. PHILLIP'S APARTMENT - NIGHT - 1990s

The bedroom is dark. Wracking coughs. The light comes on.
David turns to Phillip.

DAVID
You okay?

Phillip sweats, coughs and shakes his head as he sits.

David gets up and enters the bathroom. He returns with a
bottle of cough medicine, pills and a glass of water.

Phillip chugs from the bottle then downs two pills. He wheezes profusely.

DAVID
I want you to call the doctor first thing in the morning, okay.

PHILLIP
(raspy)
Okay.

David gets a spare pillow off a chair and props it behind Phillip's pillow.

DAVID
Christ, you're soaked.
(beat)
Get up and change. You need to stay warm and dry.

Phillip gets up and strips off his t-shirt. He puts on a clean t-shirt.

David strips the bed and remakes it.

Phillip gets back into bed and closes his eyes, exhausted.

David gets into bed and turns the light off.

LATER

Severe wracking coughs and loud wheezing.

The light comes on and David turns quickly to find Phillip struggling for breath. He grabs the phone and calls 911.

LATER

AMBULANCE ATTENDANTS lift Phillip, with oxygen in his nose, IV hook-up, onto a gurney. They wheel him out of the bedroom.

David follows, a complete nervous wreck.

INT. HOSPITAL ROOM - NIGHT - 1990s

Phillip, hooked up to monitors, IV, and oxygen, sleeps.

David sits in a chair by the bed, deep in thought.

INT. ALEX' OFFICE - DAY - 1990s

Alex and Lola compare numbers on a document. Phone rings.

> ALEX
> Alex.
> (beat)
> David, what's wrong?
> (beat)
> St. Lukes? What room? Why didn't you call me?

Alex scribbles on a note pad.

> ALEX
> I'll be there in a few minutes.

Alex stands as he hangs up the phone.

> LOLA
> What happened?

> ALEX
> Phillip's in the hospital.

LOLA

Oh my God! Was he in an accident?

ALEX

Pneumonia.

Alex exits.

INT. HOSPITAL - DAY - 1990s

Alex enters the hospital room.

David springs up from the chair and they embrace. David clings to Alex and cries.

Phillip sleeps as equipment monitors him. Alex glances at Phillip as he and David part.

ALEX

Christ. I didn't know it was this bad.

David wipes a tear.

DAVID

You know how stubborn he gets about taking medication.

Alex shakes his head.

ALEX

Is he going to be okay?

David nods vigorously.

DAVID

Doctor said he was responding well. The antibiotics are working like a charm.

Phillip stirs, opens his eyes. Alex pats Phillip's leg.

ALEX
Hey there, buddy.

Phillip smiles weakly.

PHILLIP
I know, I know. Take your damn medicine. David's already yapped my ears off.

ALEX
Damn right. Give everybody a scare like this.

DAVID
Low self esteem. Has to make sure he's the center of attention.

Phillip smiles weakly and closes his eyes.

ALEX
You get rested up.

He pats Phillip's leg again, then puts his arm across David's shoulder.

ALEX
Take care of yourself.

David and Alex sit like sentinels on each side of the bed as Phillip rests.

When it appears that Phillip is asleep, Alex quietly rises.

ALEX
Let me know what the doctor says.

David nods. They hug.

DAVID
Thanks for coming.

Alex exits.

INT. ALEX AND CHELSEA'S TOWNHOUSE - NIGHT -
1990s

Alex and Chelsea watch CNN.

Doorbell rings.

Alex answers the door.

ALEX
What brings you out this way?

Chuck enters.

CHUCK
Bought some new golf gloves.

He extends a small bag to Alex.

Alex and Chuck walk to the sofa.

CHELSEA
Shopping again?

CHUCK
I'm a stiff competitor for bargains.

They laugh.

Alex opens the bag and checks out the gloves.

ALEX
Nice.

Chuck takes the gloves and puts them on.

CHUCK
These fit perfectly.

ALEX
Think they'll improve your game?

They jostle each other.

Chelsea laughs.

CHELSEA
From what I've heard, you need help, Chuck.

CHUCK
Not all doctors are golf pro's.

ALEX
Meant to call you today. Phillip's in the hospital.

Chuck becomes serious.

CHUCK

What's wrong?

CHUCK? ...

ALEX
Pneumonia.

CHUCK
Let the bronchitis get away from him again, didn't he?

Alex nods.

CHUCK
I'll stop by and see him tomorrow.

INT. PHILLIP'S HOSPITAL ROOM - EVENING -
1990s

Chuck enters Phillip's room.

Phillip sleeps.

Chuck exits.

EXT. HOSPITAL HALLWAY - 1990s

Chuck walks toward the Nurses Station.

Doctor Adams approaches the Nurses Station from the opposite direction and gets there first.

DOCTOR ADAMS
Let me see Phillip Randall's chart.

Chuck approaches.

CHUCK
Jim, good to see you.

Doctor Adams turns to Chuck; they shake hands.

DOCTOR ADAMS
What are you doing in my territory Chuck?

CHUCK
Came to check on Phillip Randall for a friend.
How's he doing?

DOCTOR ADAMS
Damn shame.

Doctor Adams pulls Chuck aside.

CHUCK
His whole family has this bronchial condition...

DOCTOR ADAMS
You don't know?

Chuck appears perplexed.

DOCTOR ADAMS
AIDS.

Chuck keeps his composure in check.

CHUCK
Conclusive?

DOCTOR ADAMS
Yup. Got the results in my office.

CHUCK
Why isn't he on the AIDS floor?

DOCTOR ADAMS
Didn't see any reason for that at this point.

CHUCK
Never crossed my mind that he could have AIDS.

DOCTOR ADAMS
I almost fell over when he told me he was gay.

CHUCK
Oh boy. Well, thanks for the update.

DOCTOR ADAMS
Let's play a round of golf soon.

CHUCK
I'll call you.

They part.

Chuck heads back to Phillip's room.

INT. PHILLIP'S ROOM - 1990s

Chuck approaches the bed.

Phillip stirs awake, smiles weakly.

PHILLIP
Hey, Chuck.

Chuck keeps his anger under check.

CHUCK
How long have you known?

PHILLIP
Known?

CHUCK
Don't bullshit me. I just saw Doctor Adams. Does David know?
Did you tell Alex?

Phillip appears very uncomfortable.

PHILLIP
I haven't told anyone. They're not sick! I am.

Chuck clenches his fist.

CHUCK
You selfish son of a bitch. How long have you known?

PHILLIP
Just six months. I don't know how I got infected. No one I know
is sick.

CHUCK
Take a look in the mirror. You can't tell if someone is HIV
positive by looking at them.

Chuck turns to leave.

CHUCK
You'd better come clean with David or I'll tell him.

PHILLIP

When's the last time you had an AIDS test? Keep out of my
business.

Chuck approaches the bed in a threatening manner.

CHUCK

Your business includes ME...

Chuck hits his own chest.

CHUCK

Alex, Chelsea, Jason and Janie.

Phillip appears unmoved.

PHILLIP

I wasn't sick then.

CHUCK

This can go back ten, twenty years. You should have told Alex
and David the minute you found out.

PHILLIP

What difference does it make now?

CHUCK

You owe them that much.

Chuck exits the room, furious.

INT. CHUCK'S OFFICE - NIGHT - 1990s

Chuck smolders at his desk. He reaches for the phone; stops. Reaches again. Stops. He glances at the clock: 10:30.

He gets up, turns off the light and exits.

INT. ALEX' OFFICE - DAY - 1990s

Alex works on the computer. Phone rings.

> ALEX
> Alex.

INT. CHUCK'S OFFICE - DAY - 1990s

Chuck wrestles with emotions.

> CHUCK
> Can you drop what you're doing and come over?

BACK TO SCENE

Alex sits back, concerned.

> ALEX
> Sure. What's up?

INT. CHUCK'S OFFICE - DAY - 1990s

Chuck appears mentally brutalized.

> CHUCK
> We need to talk.

BACK TO SCENE

Alex tenses.

ALEX

If you're interested in seeing someone else, you can tell me over the phone.

INT. CHUCK'S OFFICE - DAY - 1990s

Chuck lightens up.

CHUCK

That will never happen.

BACK TO SCENE

Alex relaxes.

ALEX

I'll be right there.

Alex exits.

INT. CHUCK'S OFFICE - DAY - 1990s

MARY LYNN escorts Alex to Chuck's office.

CHUCK
(to Mary Lynn)
See that I'm not disturbed.

MARY LYNN
They'll have to get through me.

She closes the door as she exits.

Alex sits.

ALEX

What the hell is all this melodrama?

Chuck sits. He folds his hands, unfolds, refolds.

CHUCK

I stopped by Phillip's room last night and happened to run into his family physician.

Alex sits straight.

ALEX

Has he gotten worse? He's not dead is he?

Chuck shakes his head.

Alex exhales loudly in relief.

CHUCK

Phillip has AIDS.

Alex is blown away.

Chuck rubs his eyes, then looks up.

CHUCK

The son of a bitch has known for six months. David doesn't have a clue.

Alex takes a deep breath.

ALEX

Why didn't he say something?

CHUCK
Because he's a selfish maggot.

The phone intercom BUZZES.

CHUCK
Shit!
(presses button)
What is it?

MARY LYNN (O.S.)
There's a gentleman here that insists on seeing you.

CHUCK
Who is it?

MARY LYNN (O.S.)
David Bergstrom.

Chuck and Alex practically have an emotional meltdown.

CHUCK
Send him back.

Alex and Chuck stand.

David storms into the office.

Chuck shuts the door.

David bursts into a tirade with arms flailing in all directions.

DAVID
How long have you known?

He turns to Alex, then Chuck.

CHUCK

Alex just found out. I made the discovery last night.
(beat)
Let's stay calm... sit down and talk about this.

Alex collapses into a chair.

Chuck sits and waits expectantly for David to comply.

David reluctantly sits.

DAVID

If this gets out, my business is ruined.

ALEX

Business? What about my family? What about Chuck?

DAVID

No one told you to play it straight. That was your decision.

Alex and David are set to spring on each other.

CHUCK

Will you two settle down. I'm a doctor. You think people are
going to want me poking at them if I'm infected? Think again.

ALEX

So what are we going to do?

DAVID

Yeah, Chuck. Got any secret cures in your black bag?

CHUCK
We're going to get tested.

Alex and David stare at Chuck as he picks up the phone.

INT. AIDS TESTING CLINIC - DAY - 1990s

Alex, David and Chuck enter and approach a CLERK at the window.

CHUCK
We have an appointment with Patricia.

CLERK
Go ahead and have a seat and I'll give her a call.

Alex, Chuck and David look around and find three seats together and sit.

David, restless, gets up and walks around the room. He scans various bulletin boards with health posters.

One AIDS poster catches his eye. Several people are represented in one.

PATRICIA, a middle-aged woman, enters the room and spots Chuck.

PATRICIA
Good to see you, doctor.

Chuck and Alex get up.

David springs to her side.

She sticks her hand out toward Chuck.

PATRICIA

You keep spreading the word.

CHUCK

Thanks for getting us in together.

PATRICIA

I hate to say it, but your circumstances are not unusual. It's just a shame that people are not morally responsible these days.

Patricia leads them out of the room.

INT. HALLWAY - 1990s

They walk several yards to a room and Patricia ushers them inside.

INT. LAB ROOM - 1990s

Chuck, David and Alex sit in chairs that have an attached side table.

Patricia sits opposite them, close to a small cabinet. A clipboard sits on the side table of each chair.

PATRICIA

Typically, you'd fill out these questionnaires in the waiting room, but I told the guys you were special.

The men tackle the questions.

DAVID

Why do you ask about anal sex if you ask if we're gay?

PATRICIA

Good question, I don't rightly know.

Patricia waits patiently. The men finish.

> PATRICIA
> All done?

Patricia gathers some papers off a credenza.

> PATRICIA
> Hold on to your clipboards. You will be placing identification
> numbers on your paperwork. We have to make sure the results
> are not mixed up in the shuffle.

> ALEX
> That would not be good.

> PATRICIA
> The results will be back in twenty minutes. Did you want to
> hear your results individually or as a team?

All ponder this.

> ALEX
> I think I'd rather have my friends with me.

David and Chuck nod in agreement.

> PATRICIA
> All right.

Patricia slips a two-part form with a peel-off number on each of
their questionnaires's.

Then she gathers three OraQuick packages.

PATRICIA

OraQuick has been the greatest discovery since grilled cheese sandwiches. The results are produced almost instantaneously.

DAVID

I don't deal with needles very well.

PATRICIA

You don't have to worry about that. This is an oral test device.

David, Alex and Chuck examine the OraQuick packages.

The packages contain a plastic blue vial rack, a plastic vial, collector pad test device.

PATRICIA

I want you to write today's date under this long number.

She points to the number on the form.

The guys pull pens out of their pockets and write.

PATRICIA

Now open your packages and remove the collector pad test device.

She holds one up for them to see.

They each peel the packets open and pull out the device.

PATRICIA

Okay, now put the collector pad in your mouth and rub it
around to get your saliva on it.

Alex, Chuck and David follow directions.

PATRICIA

Now just hold it there. You can close your mouth. I'm going to
time this for three minutes.

She glances at her watch.

All three guys sit with the sticks protruding from their closed
mouths.

A timer DINGS from her watch or phone.

PATRICIA

Times up. Pick up the vial and open it. Take the collector pad
and place it in the vial.

They remove the caps on the vial and stick the collector pads
into the vials.

PATRICIA

You guys follow directions real well.
(beat)
I suggest that you go back out to the waiting room so you don't
sit here and stare at the OraQuick for the results.

CHUCK

Now to get through the next twenty minutes.

The men stand. They exit out the door.

INT. WAITING ROOM - DAY - 1990s

Alex finds concentration impossible as he flips through a magazine. He gets up and walks around.

Alex, Chuck and David sit ramrod straight with their arms crossed in front of them.

Patricia enters with BRUCE, a big brute of a guy.

> PATRICIA
> This is my assistant, Bruce.

Nods only.

> PATRICIA
> Let's go back and get your results.

INT. LAB ROOM -- DAY - 1990s

Patricia, Bruce, Alex, David and Chuck file into the room.

Patricia motions for the men to sit in their chairs.

The blue vial holder is turned away from each of the men.

> PATRICIA
> Please do not turn your test kit around just yet.
> (beat)
> Is the paperwork in front of you yours?

All check and nod.

Patricia turns to David, turns his test kit around and points to two pink lines on the collector pad test device.

PATRICIA

Do you see these two pink lines? Your test shows reactive, which means HIV antibodies were found in your sample.

David explodes out of the chair.

DAVID

How could he do this to me?

Bruce springs to his feet and grabs David in a bear hug.

Chuck and Alex jump up and hover close by.

David cries - racking sobs.

Bruce releases David to Alex and Chuck. They sit back down.

Patricia gives Chuck the news next as she turns his kit toward him.

PATRICIA

Do you see that there is only one pink line? Your test came back non reactive. I suggest that you have regular tests to be on the safe side

Chuck lets out a sigh of relief.

PATRICIA

You do realize that because you are a doctor, we have to report this?

CHUCK

But I'm non reactive.

PATRICIA

For the moment. It could show up anytime... your patients could be at risk.

Chuck appears ashen.

Alex sits, tense.

Patricia turns Alex's test kit around. Two lines are clearly visible.

PATRICIA
Your test came back reactive.

Alex sits in shock.

Patricia addresses David and Alex.

PATRICIA
We should immediately draw blood and verify these findings. Do you want to do that while you're here?

Both nod, numb.

INT. CHUCK'S OFFICE - DAY - 1990s

Alex enters Chuck's office and closes the door.

Chuck appears drained.

Alex collapses in a chair.

EXT. CEMETERY - DAY - CURRENT DAY

The birds chirp during a lull in the ceremony as the Priest continues.

Chuck holds Janie.

Alex stands statue still.

Chelsea whispers to Jason.

David cries softly.

Donna stands with eyes closed.

BACK TO SCENE

                    CHUCK
It's only a matter of time before it shows up. I'll have to get
              tested every couple of months.

A long silence.

                    ALEX
              Have you talked to David?

                    CHUCK
If he continues his workouts and eating practices, he'll do
alright. He'll have to leave the cooking and food preparation to
         his employees, but he'll keep his business.

Alex nods, lost in shock.

                    ALEX
              What about me?

Chuck breaths deeply, swelling with emotion.

                    CHUCK
You appear outwardly healthy. I'd suggest increasing your odds
         by living healthier than ever.

ALEX
Chelsea and the kids?

CHUCK
They'll have to be tested.

Alex stares at the floor.

ALEX
Right away?

CHUCK
Get it over with.

After a short while, Alex stands.

Chuck gets up.

ALEX
Not yet. I need to think.

Chuck nods.

Alex goes to the door and stops. He turns and they embrace.

Chuck cries.

Alex fights back tears.

INT. PHILLIP'S APARTMENT - DAY - 1990s

David opens the door and Alex enters. They embrace emotionally.

DAVID
How are you?

Alex nods, gravely.

> ALEX
> How's he doing?

> DAVID
> Not much better. He's dropping pounds.

Alex enters Phillip's room.

Phillip appears to be asleep in a hospital-type bed.

Alex sits in the chair beside the bed. He stares at Phillip.

Phillip stirs. He opens his eyes and sees Alex.

> PHILLIP
> (wheezes heavily)
> You came.
> (beat, difficult breathing)
> I know you must hate me.

> ALEX
> You don't know anything about me. You never did.

> PHILLIP
> Always the brooding thinker.

> ALEX
> Why didn't you tell me, Phillip? We have a fifteen year history.
> Didn't you think I deserved to know?

Phillip coughs. He raises the head of his bed.

PHILLIP
I didn't think it mattered. You're never sick...

ALEX
Jesus! Don't you ever read the papers? People die from this
every day. You don't have to look sick to be sick.

PHILLIP
Spare me the lecture.

ALEX
Spare you shit.

Alex stands abruptly and exits.

PHILLIP
Alex! Alex!

Phillip struggles to get up and falls back, exhausted.

David stands in the doorway, head hung sadly.

INT. ALEX AND CHELSEA'S TOWNHOUSE - NIGHT -
1990s

Alex enters the apartment, worn out.

Chelsea sits on the sofa reading. She appears to be angry, but
her demeanor changes when she sees him.

CHELSEA
What's wrong? Where have you been?

Alex sinks into the other end of the sofa.

ALEX
I went to see Phillip.

CHELSEA
How is he?

Alex closes his eyes.

ALEX
He has AIDS.

Chelsea cannot hide her shock.

CHELSEA
What? I thought he had pneumonia... from the bronchitis.

Alex cannot look at her.

ALEX
It's one of the symptoms. There are dozens of symptoms.

They sit in shocked silence.

Chelsea propels herself to Alex. She holds him.

CHELSEA
Oh, God. This is terrible. You must be devastated.

Alex holds her without emotion -- shell shocked from the entire experience.

They part.

Chelsea holds Alex' hand.

CHELSEA
Have you talked to Chuck?

ALEX
Briefly.

CHELSEA
Did Phillip get a blood transfusion that was bad?

Alex extracts his hand from hers.

ALEX
Blood?

CHELSEA
You know. Did he get AIDS from bad blood?

ALEX
Chelsea, Phillip is gay.

Chelsea's mouth flies open.

CHELSEA
Phillip -- gay?

Chelsea stares at Alex in disbelief. Alex nods.

CHELSEA
You knew this all along?

Alex nods.

CHELSEA

Why didn't you tell me?

ALEX

That would have been violating a confidence of friendship.
(beat)
Does it make any difference in the way you feel about him?

CHELSEA

Well... no, but I would have liked to have known.

Alex gets up and goes to the kitchen. Chelsea follows.

ALEX

He wanted his privacy.

CHELSEA

Maybe so, but he never had the opportunity to talk about dates,
fun times with lovers or anything.

Alex grabs a beer out of the fridge. He passes one to Chelsea
and grabs one for himself.

ALEX

Maybe he didn't want to share that information.

CHELSEA

Did he talk to you about it?

Alex opens his beer and slugs down a mouthful. He nods.

ALEX

We've been friends since high school. It never made any
difference to me.

Chelsea opens her beer and takes a sip. They return to the living room.

CHELSEA
Donna will just die! She had a thing for him all through school.

ALEX
Well now you know why he couldn't get it up.

CHELSEA
I wonder what his type is?

ALEX
David.

Chelsea spurts out a mouthful of beer.

CHELSEA
Oh my God! You must think I'm the most naive person on the planet. I can't believe I never figured this out before.

ALEX
There, now you have the full scoop.

Janie and Jason run into the room.

JANIE/JASON
Daddy! Daddy!

Alex scoops them up in his arms and crushes them to him.

INT. CHUCK'S HI-RISE - NIGHT - 1990s

Chuck sits on a sofa and stares out at the illuminated skyline over the balcony, drink in hand.

Pictures of Alex, Chelsea and the kids decorate a table.

Chuck picks up a picture of Alex and cries.

INT. SPLIT SCREEN -- ALEX' OFFICE -- CHUCK'S OFFICE - 1990s

Alex closes the door and makes a phone call.

ALEX
Hi Mary Lynn, Is Chuck busy?
(beat)
Hi.

Chuck leans back in his chair.

CHUCK
Have you told her yet?

ALEX
I told her about Phillip last night.

CHUCK
You've got to tell her.

ALEX
I'm getting there.

Chuck rubs his eyes, weary.

CHUCK
Alex...

Both hang up phones.

INT. ALEX AND CHELSEA'S TOWNHOUSE - DAY - 1990s

SUPER: SIX MONTHS LATER

Jason and Janie play in the living room while Chelsea reads on the sofa.

The front door opens and Alex and Chuck enter. Alex sets his golf bag inside the door.

The kids run squealing to the men.

> JASON
> Uncle Chuck!

> JANIE
> Daddy!

Chuck scoops up Jason and Alex grabs Janie and smothers her in kisses.

She squeals in delight.

Alex kisses Chelsea.

Phone rings.

Chelsea grabs the phone.

> CHELSEA
> Hello?

She listens and covers the mouth piece.

> CHELSEA
It's David. Phillip's in the hospital again.

Alex hurries around the sofa to the phone.

Chelsea hands him the phone.

> ALEX
David? You okay?
(to Chuck)
He collapsed?

Chuck nods his head, sadly. He puts his arm around Chelsea's shoulder and squeezes, in comfort.

Chelsea is visibly upset.

> CHELSEA
(to Chuck)
He's going to die, isn't he?

She screws up her face, trying not to cry.

Chuck steers her away from the phone.

> CHUCK
He's very ill.

Chelsea cries softly.

Chuck holds her.

> CHELSEA
I feel sorry for Alex. You know, he never judged Phillip.

Chuck's face tightens.

> CHUCK
> Alex accepts all situations. He's one of a kind.

Alex hangs up the phone.

> ALEX
> I'd better go stay with David.

Chelsea breaks away from Chuck.

> CHELSEA
> Is he at the hospital?

Alex nods.

> CHUCK
> I'll drive.

Alex and Chelsea embrace heavily.

Chelsea cries.

> CHELSEA
> Be brave.

They part. Alex kisses her forehead. He and Chuck exit.

INT. HOSPITAL - DAY - 1990s

David paces outside a hospital room door.

Alex and Chuck approach. David springs to Alex.

DAVID
He's dying. What am I going to do?

Alex and Chuck try to calm David.

ALEX
What do you mean, exactly?

CHUCK
I know this staff; he'll get the very best of care.

David calms.

DAVID
They've done all these things to him.

CHUCK
What things?

DAVID
He couldn't breathe. They stuck a tube in his throat.

ALEX
(to Chuck)
That's common, isn't it?

Chuck nods.

CHUCK
Phillip is a very sick man, David. He's not going to recover.
We've known that for some time now.

Alex propels David to the room door.

ALEX
Ready?

David nods. They enter the room.

INT. HOSPITAL ROOM

Phillip, thin and frail, breathes with difficulty as Alex, Chuck and David stand close to the bed.

Phillip opens his eyes. He smiles at Alex.

Alex takes Phillip's hand and smiles weakly.

ALEX
Hi.

PHILLIP
Alex. You came.

ALEX
I'll always be here for you, Phillip.

PHILLIP
(to Chuck)
You'll have to take care of him now.

Alex suppresses a choking cry.

CHUCK
I will; I promise.

David hovers close by.

Phillip blows David a kiss.

PHILLIP
My sweet, sweet boy.

Phillip dies.

Alex and David cling together in grief.

Chuck holds both.

INT. ALEX AND CHELSEA'S TOWNHOUSE - NIGHT -
1990s

Chelsea reads on the sofa.

Alex enters.

Chelsea springs off the sofa and goes to him. They embrace
heavily.

ALEX
He's gone, Chelsea.

Both cry.

Alex holds her tight and stares straight ahead.

ALEX
Chelsea, I tested positive.

Chelsea stiffens in Alex's arms. She tries to pull away, but he
has a firm embrace.

CHELSEA
Positive? How... Andrea?

She forces herself out of his arms.

They square off. She looks at him in disbelief. Tears stream down Alex' cheeks.

He shakes his head.

ALEX
Phillip.

CHELSEA
Phillip? All this time I was so worried about Andrea. How could I have been so stupid... so completely naive!

Chelsea is shell shocked.

ALEX
It was... in college, then I met you...

CHELSEA
How long have you known?

ALEX
Six months.

CHELSEA
Six months! Why didn't you tell me?

She pounds on him.

He puts his hands up trying to fend off her hits.

ALEX
I just couldn't accept that a brief situation could have this type of results.

CHELSEA

Alex! Our children. What about our children? What about
me... my career?

ALEX

Everyone will have to be tested.

CHELSEA

You selfish son of a bitch! How could you keep this to yourself?

ALEX

Watching Phillip slowly die was too painful.

CHELSEA

Alex I've loved you, devoted myself to you, bore your children...
how could you betray me like this? Our marriage is a complete
sham!

Alex reaches out to Chelsea.

ALEX

No... no it isn't.

Chelsea erupts with blind rage.

CHELSEA

Get out of this house!

ALEX

Chelsea, please...

Chelsea storms to the bedroom.

INT. BEDROOM - NIGHT - 1990s

Chelsea bursts into the bedroom followed shortly by Alex.

Chelsea yanks open the closet.

She emerges with a suitcase and throws it on the bed. She opens the suitcase, then proceeds to jerk open drawers and dumps Alex' clothes inside.

ALEX
Chelsea, don't shut me out now. Not now.

CHELSEA
You may have murdered my children with your secret, you selfish, lying bastard.

She enters the closet and returns with a couple of suits on hangers and shoves them into Alex' chest.

ALEX
They have new treatments. People are living with this.
Chelsea stops and looks Alex squarely in the eyes.

CHELSEA
And that makes it okay in your eye? It's not as big of a deal as I make it out to be because of the new drugs?
(beat)
I'll be on the phone with Donna, as my attorney, just as soon as you leave.

ALEX
Donna? You really think you need a lawyer for this?

Chelsea stops for a moment, then sucks in her breath.

CHELSEA
Oh my God. Jason has the same symptoms as Phillip!

Chelsea hurries from the room in tears.

Alex sinks onto the bed in shock.

ALEX
No, no, no... it can't be!

INT. CHUCK'S OFFICE - DAY - 1990s

Chelsea sits in front of Chuck's desk, numb.

Chuck appears to have aged ten years.

CHUCK
You know the law as well as I do. I have to report this. You're a
dentist.

CHELSEA
But I'm non reactive... negative, Chuck. It's not fair. He's ruined
my life, my son's life. How long before Jason becomes really ill?

Chuck shakes his head.

CHUCK
The best thing to do is set up a schedule for you and Janie to be
tested every six months. We'll have to find Jason the best
pediatric specialist and begin a treatment plan.

CHELSEA

You know, I've wanted to be a dentist ever since I was six years old. All my dreams washed away with this one-time liaison.

Chuck appears to say something but stops, catches himself. He sits quiet for a moment.

CHUCK
Don't keep Alex from the kids, Chelsea. He loves them and you more than life.

CHELSEA
Is he going to die?

CHUCK
Not if I can help it.

EXT. CEMETERY - DAY - CURRENT DAY

Alex, head bent, eyes closed, rests his lips on Jason's head.

PRIEST (B.G.)
God of holiness and power, accept
our prayers on behalf of your servant Phillip; do not count his deeds against him, for in his heart he desired to do your will.

Alex looks up and stares at the coffin.

PRIEST (B.G.)
As his faith united him to your people on earth, so may your mercy join him to the angels in heaven.

Alex looks at Chelsea and the kids.

ALEX
(under his breath)
What have I done?

PRIEST (B.G.)
We ask this through Christ our Lord.
(beat)
Amen.

ALL MOURNERS
Amen.

David cries softly.

Alex embraces David then turns to hug Chelsea. She turns away from him.

Chelsea embraces David.

Chuck encircles Alex, Chelsea and David in his arms.

Chelsea extricates herself. With Janie in her arms, she clutches Jason's tiny hand and leads him to the car.

Alex follows.

They enter separate cars.

INT. DONNA'S OFFICE - DAY - CURRENT DAY

SUPER - SIX MONTHS LATER

Donna comforts Chelsea on a sofa in her plush office.

DONNA
I have the divorce petition ready. Alex and his lawyer have

agreed to all the medical stipulations and special provisions we
talked about.
(beat)
When do you start teaching?

CHELSEA
In the fall. Thank God UT had an opening.

DONNA
They would have made room for you Chelsea. Your dad is a
major supporter, and it didn't do you any harm being in the top
five percentile of your class.

CHELSEA
When's the court date?

DONNA
January 17.

Chelsea nods.

INT. CHELSEA'S NEW HOUSE - SAN ANTONIO, TX -
NIGHT CURRENT DAY

SUPER - ONE YEAR LATER

Chelsea sits at a desk in her office, reading papers. Phone rings.

CHELSEA
Hello? David! How are you? This weekend? Yes. Come on up!
Ok. See you then.

EXT. CHELSEA'S HOUSE - DAY - CURRENT DAY

A car pulls up and parks.

David exits and walks up the path.

The door bursts open and Jason (6) and Janie (4) rush out to greet him, Chelsea in the rear.

> JANIE/JASON
> Uncle David!

David squats, arms wide and gathers them in a hug and kisses them.

> DAVID
> Look at you two. You're so big! When did you get this big?
> Have you been eating those climbing green beans?

The kids laugh. They run back to the house.

David stands.

He and Chelsea come together in a tight embrace. They part, a little teary.

> CHELSEA
> I'm so glad you're here. I've missed you so much.

> DAVID
> I've missed you too.

They walk to the house.

> DAVID
> I'm looking at restaurant space on the River Walk.
> Chelsea stops, thrilled.

CHELSEA

Oh this is wonderful! I'll have my best friend-chef back?

David nods.

DAVID

Taking over the town.

INT. CHELSEA'S BEDROOM - NIGHT - CURRENT DAY

SUPER - ONE YEAR LATER

Chelsea sleeps peacefully as moonlight cascades across the floor.

O.S. Wracking coughs shatter the silence.

Chelsea bolts up in bed, then bursts out of the bed and out of the room.

INT. JASON'S ROOM - CURRENT DAY

Jason coughing stops. He wheezes dangerously, trying to suck in air.

Chelsea has the portable phone.

CHELSEA

I need an ambulance for my son. He can't breathe!

INT. HOSPITAL - NIGHT - CURRENT DAY

Chelsea sits with David, ready to explode off the sofa.

Alex and Chuck approach.

Chuck appears a little older, Alex, thinner but healthy.

ALEX
We got here as soon as we could. Is Jason alright?

Chelsea appears bitter.

CHELSEA
This is all your fault!

Chuck comes to Chelsea and puts his arm around her as she cries.

CHUCK
We'll get through this. Who's the doctor?

Chelsea looks at David.

He shakes his head.

CHELSEA
I can't remember. It all happened so fast.

Chuck talks quietly.

CHUCK
I'll go find out what's going on. You just wait here.

Chuck gets up and walks down the hall and disappears.

Alex sits, lost in thought.

MONTAGE:

Chelsea sitting by Jason's side, stroking his hair, in a hospital room.

Alex sitting with Jason, crying silently as he watches Jason's small form, tubes in his nose, in the hospital room.

Chuck grimly checking Jason's vital signs.

David and Chuck in the waiting room.

LATER

Chelsea and Alex are at Jason's bedside as he struggles for breath.

Chelsea presses the nurse's call button frantically.

> ALEX
> Nurse! Nurse!

Chuck and David rush in.

Moments later, a MEDICAL TEAM rushes in.

Chuck and David pry Chelsea and Alex out of the room as Chelsea struggles to stay behind.

> CHELSEA
> Is he going to be alright?

INT. WAITING ROOM - CURRENT DAY

David holds Chelsea.

Alex and Chuck huddle.

The Doctor approaches. He shakes his head.

Chelsea WAILS.

Alex crumbles.

All cry.

EXT. CEMETERY - DAY - CURRENT DAY

The Priest and much of the same crowd that attended Phillip's funeral stands as the small coffin is lowered into the ground.

Chelsea, wrecked with anguish, is flanked by Janie, Donna, David and her parents.

Alex, devastated, is supported by his parents, Chuck and Lola.

                              PRIEST
        Let us pray for those who mourn. Comfort them in their grief.
               Lord, in your mercy - hear our prayer.

                                                    FADE OUT.

Screenwriter, Editor, Author, Writing Coach, Publisher, Retired Technical Writer. Creator of worlds and characters. I do it all. I win awards. I can fix yours.

D.E. Greenfield, Dawn Greenfield Ireland, also known as DG Ireland, is an award-winning author of 21 novels, including 5 series (cozy mystery, sci fi/fantasy, billionaire shapeshifters, and dystopian), and a stand-alone sci-fi romantic adventure.

Most of her 7 nonfiction books have won awards. Dawn has adapted a few of her screenplays into book format, and several of her books into TV series format. She also created over 50 themed notebooks.

Two of her screenplays were optioned and she worked on a screenwriter-for-hire project. Dawn has a certificate from the Professional Program in Screenwriting from UCLA (2002), and a certificate from ScreenwritingU (2023).

Dawn writes full time. She lives among dreams and fantasies with two cats and moving boxes. Her head is filled with stories. She doesn't suffer from writer's block.

Her business, Artistic Origins, has been around since 1995. Besides writing, she coaches writers, edits, formats and publishes clients' books.

Her former day job as an award-winning technical writer played a major role in her fiction writing. She is detailed-oriented, the organizational queen of the known universe, and never misses a deadline.

https://amazon.com/author/dawnireland

https://facebook.com/dawn.ireland.18

https://x.com/dawnireland

https://instagram.com/dawngreenfieldIreland

https://goodreads.com/dawnireland

https://linkedin.com/in/degreenfield

https://tiktok.com/@writerg4l